DOCTOR WHO

THE CHURCH ON RUBY ROAD

THE CHURCH ON RUBY ROAD

Based on the BBC television adventure
by Russell T Davies

ESMIE JIKIEMI-PEARSON

BOOKS

BBC Books, an imprint of Ebury Publishing
20 Vauxhall Bridge Road,
London SW1V 2SA

BBC Books is part of the Penguin Random House group of companies
whose addresses can be found at global.penguinrandomhouse.com

Doctor Who is produced in Wales by Bad Wolf
with BBC Studios Productions

Executive Producers: Jane Tranter, Julie Gardner, Joel Collins,
Phil Collinson and Russell T Davies

First published by BBC Books in 2024

www.penguin.co.uk

A CIP catalogue record for this book is available from the British Library

ISBN 9781785948695

Editorial Director: Albert DePetrillo
Project Editor: Steve Cole
Cover Design: Lee Binding

Typeset by Rocket Editorial Ltd
Printed and bound in Great Britain by Clays Ltd, Elcograf S.p.A.

The authorised representative in the EEA is Penguin Random House Ireland,
Morrison Chambers, 32 Nassau Street, Dublin D02 YH68

Contents

To my dear parents, Pamela and Adam,
for always encouraging me to dream big.

Chapter One

Manchester, 24 December, 2004

Once upon a time, late on Christmas Eve, a stranger came to the church on Ruby Road.

It was an old church, the grand kind one usually finds in small villages, with a tower and a clockface. Gravestones stood in the front churchyard: great stone crosses made blurry and indistinct by the snow which fell in heavy flakes from the night sky, blanketing the whole scene in white, muffling the sounds of the stranger's frantic footsteps. Beyond the church, in the middle distance, houses stretched out in neat rows, their windows flickering with warm light.

But in the churchyard, the only illumination came from old-fashioned streetlamps, the sort you might read about in a children's story, their yellow light struggling out from behind dusty panes.

Indeed, you might be forgiven for thinking *this* is a children's story. Alas, it is not.

The stranger was dressed for snow – wrapped in a shawl all the way up to her eyes and ears, shuffling down the icy street, and clutching a bundle in her hands. She might have wanted to stop and catch her breath, but she gave

1

no sign of it. The stranger just kept walking, her precious bundle pressed to her chest as she made her way towards the church. Determined, steady.

When she reached the grand, arching wooden doors, she placed the bundle before them, on the ground. In the light of the streetlamp, her daughter's face was visible, peeking out of the swaddling blankets, a pale circle with a button nose, eyes squeezed shut.

Above her, the minute hand on the clocktower ticked closer to the hour.

By the time it struck midnight, the stranger was gone, swallowed by the snow and the dark of the night, vanished completely into the wideness of the world.

Had the stranger turned back, perhaps to raise her hand in farewell to her daughter, she would have seen the door open just as the rolling tolls of the church bell rang the hour, a flood of light and warmth like a river spilling across the stone, the merry sound of the choir carrying out into the freezing air of the night. She would have watched from afar as the vicar glanced around, his face wrinkling at the sight of the bundle on the doorstep. The small, waving hands, the little nose and wisps of blonde hair peeking out from beneath the child's little cap. She would have seen him scoop up the child, his robes ruffling in the cold evening air, before shaking his head, and placing a kiss on the newborn's brow.

But the stranger did not see any of those things, though she might have, if only she had turned. Instead, she moved forward, onward, and disappeared into the snow.

Now, if this were a true Christmas fairy tale, the stranger might have been reunited with her daughter, many years later. She might have been a rich duchess, or a pirate queen, or a snow fairy come to take her child back to her icy realm. But this story isn't a fairy tale, and the stranger was never seen again. No one ever even knew her name.

This is what happened instead.

Across the snowy square, frozen still as a statue, was a man. In the darkness, his long coat shrouded him in shadow. Behind him, a blue police box stood in the snow, its door open, the interior glowing softly. The man's sad, clever eyes followed the stranger down the road, watching as she hurried off; a hooded figure, dark and lonely against the snow, which had begun to fall heavier and heavier, piling in small drifts by the side of the road. For one moment, it seemed as though he might call to her. Say something. But the man wasn't here for her, and the mere minutes he had left to do what he needed were trickling away. Something had gone wrong in the future, terribly wrong, and the cracks in time had chased him all the way back to this night. To this very corner, on the street named Ruby Road.

The Doctor turned towards the church.

Its thin, pointed spire was gothic in the soft glow of the streetlamps, and as he stood, seen by no one, like a lonely statue amongst the falling snow, the light caught his face. And his eyes were filled with tears.

Chapter Two

'…And that's my name.' Ruby smiled, trying not to squint against the harsh glare of the lights they'd set up around her to illuminate the scene, even though they were so bright she felt like her face – along with all the makeup that had been put on it – was melting off. 'Ruby, named after Ruby Road, where I was found. Almost nineteen years ago, now.'

Shifting in her seat, she looked across at Davina McCall – Davina McCall, for god's sake, a proper famous TV presenter! – who was currently perched on a seat facing her, and wondered not for the first time if this was all an elaborate hallucination.

Ruby had grown up watching shows where celebrity hosts helped children in the care system to track down their birth families, but never in a million years did she think she'd ever go on one. The thought of staring down a camera lens and sharing all the things that had happened to her since she was found by a vicar on the steps of a church – basically, explaining her whole life – made her feel vaguely sick with anxiety.

And yet here she was.

Davina shook her dark, glossy hair and nodded under-standingly. 'So, you were a foundling. And you were fostered by Carla, who then adopted you, is that right?'

At the mention of her mum's name, Ruby felt herself relax. Carla had given her a stern talking to before she'd come on the show. *Your story belongs to you. Don't let anyone tell it for you,* she'd said before squeezing Ruby in a hug so tight she'd thought she might burst.

'Yeah, my mum's amazing.' Ruby laughed. 'I mean, she's *completely* nuts. But she's the best mum I could ever have, yeah.' She wanted to say, *Without her, I don't know what I'd do. Where I'd be. I love her more than anything.* But the words felt too personal for the glitzy London club where the interview was being filmed. The seats at the black marble bar were velvet, for crying out loud. A drink here probably cost more money than Ruby earned working two entire hours at her part-time job.

'So life's been good, would you say?' Davina asked.

'Well! Not bad. I mean, we've had the pandemic, of course, and the recession, and the Giggle.' She ticked things off her on her fingers. 'And my A levels weren't the best, cos we had to leave Manchester and move down here. We came to look after my gran – she wouldn't move north, not in a million years! And we couldn't pay for care. So that's been tricky,' she laughed awkwardly. 'And *expensive.*'

Davina nodded sagely again. 'I bet! No one moves to London these days!'

She was a good interviewer, Ruby thought. Kind, and calm. *I keep forgetting I'm on camera.* 'To be honest, it's left me a bit stranded, really. I think, well to be honest, I think I'm still waiting for my life to begin—'

'Sorry – sorry, can we stop?' A male voice interrupted her. One of the sound guys. He was frowning at his monitor, pressing his set of headphones tighter to his head, as though trying to listen in on a very faint sound. 'Is there a radio or something? I'm getting a noise – like a whisper. Could be an open door?'

Ruby blinked, the chic surroundings of the bar around her coming back into focus. Crystal lights and crystal glasses, the assembled crew, all linked via headsets and wires. She'd been so immersed in the interview that the interruption felt like a splash of cold water to the face.

Davina leaned forward conspiratorially, 'Don't worry, stuff like this happens all the time, won't take long.' She shuffled her notes. 'Oh, you don't mind me using the word "foundling", do you? Some people think it sounds a bit old-fashioned.' She smiled brightly. 'Like a fairy tale.'

Ruby shook her head. 'No, I don't mind. It's what I am.' Honestly, she didn't. Davina was right, it did sound a tad old-fashioned and maybe a little strange, but what was life without a little strangeness? She laughed. 'I *was* found. I was foundled!'

Davina eyes crinkled in a smile. 'I *love* that.'

At a signal from the sound guy, Davina beamed at Ruby again. 'Wonderful. Right, everything seems to have been sorted. Let's pick it up at… So! Ruby! The whole point of this show is to see if we can help you reconnect with your family…'

There was a small, flickering movement out of the corner of Ruby's eye. Trying her best to focus on the interview, she blinked hard. But it flickered into view again. A small grey shape. She blinked again. *Probably a wire moving, or someone's shoe,* she told herself, and refocused her attention on Davina.

'…In the old days, foundlings were left without a trace, and there was nothing we could do. But now we can work magic with DNA. We've taken your swabs and we can start the search…'

The flicker was back. And now there was a sound, like hissing, right at the limits of her hearing. Ruby tried to concentrate on Davina's face, or even just her voice, but the strange, eerie sound cut right through.

Darting a look at the sound guy, she noticed he was frowning again, looking at his monitor in confusion. Could he hear it too?

Snicker-snacker-ticker-tacker.

'Now, Ruby,' Davina was saying. Ruby wrenched her focus back to the interview. The sound faded to nothing, disappearing as swiftly as it had interrupted her. Relief flooded through her. She needed to stay present; this could be her only chance of ever tracking down her birth parents. She couldn't afford to be distracted by vague, whispering noises.

'We can't promise miracles,' Davina continued. 'And even if we *do* make contact with someone, your mum or dad, or even a cousin, they might not want to be found. And we have to respect that.'

Ruby nodded, smiling. 'I understand.'

'Can I ask, if we find someone... what are you hoping for?'

'Just the truth,' Ruby said, and she meant it. 'I mean, I don't think I'm from royalty or anything!' She laughed, but Davina didn't, just kept staring at her, earnestly, as if waiting for Ruby to elaborate. 'I just think... if I'm waiting for my life to begin, then knowing where I came from is a good place to start.'

In the back of the room, unseen by everyone, including Ruby, a thin grey hand reached towards a cup of coffee, recently set down by one of the crew. Spidery fingers wrapped around the cardboard and moved the coffee a few inches to the left, quiet as a whisper, subtle as a breeze.

The lines on the sound monitor jumped, pinging upward, picking up the faintest murmur. A hiss, barely audible. *Snicker-snacker-ticker-tacker.*

Another hand. *There!* By a plug in the wall, disconnecting it from the socket.

At the front of the room, Ruby and Davina chatted away, none the wiser.

Then several unexplainable things happened within the space of only a few seconds.

The thin grey hand pulled the wire taut, lifting it off the ground just as the crewmember noticed her coffee had inexplicably moved. She stepped forward to get it, careful not to make a sound and disturb the set, which was silent but for the sound of Davina and Ruby's voices.

The wire, pulled taut by the tiny hand, bowed against her foot as it snagged her at the ankle. There was a moment of stillness, in which the crewmember's eyes widened, her mouth opening in shock, before she toppled over, coming down hard against the floor with an almighty crash. The lid of her coffee flew off, hot liquid arcing through the air, and the wire, which was wrapped around the lamps surrounding Davina and Ruby snapped tighter…

All this happened behind Ruby, while she waited for Davina's next question, blinking in the bright lights, which seemed almost to wobble before her eyes…

'Look out!' Davina cried.

SMASH!

The wobbling lamps teetered and then fell like giant steel dominoes, crashing into each other in a shower of bright sparks and shattering glass, their wires whipping around like tentacles. Ruby yelled and dived off the stool, just as the third lamp smashed into the soft padded seat, the burning hot bulb thudding into the barstool right where she'd been sitting only moments ago.

'Oh my god!' Davina was also crouched on the ground, right where she'd landed after jumping out of the way. Her voice was shaking, her perfect hair now in disarray. 'Are you okay?'

'I'm fine!' Ruby said, taking a deep breath. 'I'm okay.' But all she could think was, *That lamp fell right where I'd been sitting. I could have been killed!* She noticed that her hands were shaking, nervous tremors caused by adrenalin. The room swam, and she shook her head to dispel the buzzing of her fear. 'I'm fine, honestly. It's okay, it missed.'

Davina's relief was palpable. 'Oh, how lucky,' she exclaimed, standing up. 'Thank goodness, I mean—'

Ruby didn't see the wire whipping around until it was too late. The plug connecting the third lamp to the wall *popped* out of the socket, a final freak event in this destructive and illogical sequence. It flew upwards, the hard plastic casing whacking Davina firmly in the back of her head with a solid *thunk*.

'Ow!' Davina cried, her hands flying up on reflex to feel for an injury. She swayed on her feet, expression woozy and disorientated, before her eyes fluttered shut, and she fell right into Ruby's arms.

Chapter Three

London, 22 December, 2023

The pub was warm, the smell of mulled wine filling the room with the undeniable spirit of Christmas.

Ruby and her band were performing their usual Christmas set, full of old classics and crowd-pleasers, with some newer, cooler Christmas anthems snuck in. The rosy-cheeked patrons laughed and chatted, coats unbuttoned, bobble hats hanging off chairs, scarves trailing forgotten on the floor. Behind the bar, a boy Ruby knew from around the area served drinks with a cheerful smile, a tinsel crown in his hair.

She could see it all from where she stood on the stage, her fingers dancing across the keyboard, its chimes mingling with the sounds of conversations and her bandmate's instruments. At the front of the stage, one of Ruby's best mates Trudy swayed, her long brown hair pin straight as usual, mic grasped in both hands, as she sang her way through a lively version of 'Winter Wonderland'. Their other bandmate, Clark, strummed at his guitar, eyes closed, cradling it as lovingly as if he wanted to take it home to cuddle up to and watch old David Attenborough documentaries. Big Jim was light on the drums, sticks flashing daintily over the cymbal, summoning a shimmering, glittering noise out of the drum set that was so Christmassy, it made Ruby feel like a kid again.

She smiled as she played her part, the noise in her head going quiet – all her usual worries disappearing, drowned out by the sound of Christmas cheer.

These were her friends. Her bandmates.

And yeah, this was only a small gig, and they'd not been paid much… But Ruby could use the money, and Trudy still had bits of tinsel in her hair from where Ruby had wrestled a tinsel scarf onto her before getting on stage, causing Clark's David Bowie eyeliner to smudge from laughing so hard at the two of them and their tinsel war that he had cried. On a cold night during the festive season, there was nowhere else she'd rather be than this cosy pub with her best friends, making music.

They all geared up for the next verse, and though the crowd wasn't paying them too much attention, they launched into it, Trudy's dreamy voice filling the room.

Out of the corner of Ruby's eye, she saw a flash of grey.

Snicker-snacker-chitter-chatter.

Distracted, her fingers stumbled over the chords.

Without warning, the music died. Trudy's microphone stopped working with a high-pitched squeal of feedback that had the whole pub groaning and covering their ears.

For a moment, all the conversation died, fifty pairs of eyes blinking up at the silent stage. Ruby stared back, her face going red, before most people shrugged and turned back to their conversations.

'What's going on?' Clark whispered.

'I don't know!' Ruby said, tapping her keyboard. There was no response. 'It's dead!' She saw Clark fiddling with his silent guitar amp. A fuse must have blown somewhere – that was the only explanation she could think of.

Trudy shouted over the noise of the crowd, 'Sorry, everyone! Trouble with the sound, we'll be back in a moment.'

A woman heckled from the bar. She looked like a bit of a hippy, Ruby thought, with a bohemian-style red headband, holding back frizzy blonde curls. 'Give it some welly!' she shouted.

'All right, I said sorry, okay!' Trudy bellowed. She was definitely the mouthy one in the group. Ruby hid a smile behind her hand.

'Give us a bit of Steeleye Span!' the woman in the headband shouted. 'Can you do "Gaudete"?'

'We don't take requests!' Trudy retorted.

Ruby shook her head. It wouldn't be a night out with the band if something didn't go even a little wrong. But they'd figure it out.

They always did.

At the back of the room, a man in a long coat watched the band from under the brim of his Bolero hat.

The pub was busy with the Christmas season, everyone standing shoulder to shoulder, packed like sardines. But the dense crowd seemed to part around him, like he was standing still in the rushing current of a river. The warm lights played across his skin, his brown eyes glittering as the corners of his mouth lifting in a smile, knowing and wise.

Ruby didn't see him. But he saw her.

Chapter Four

Music pounded through the nightclub, reverberating through Ruby's feet as she sat, watching the dancefloor. It was a crush, about 200 people swaying to the music, jumping up and down, screaming, laughing, singing along to the latest, catchiest top ten hit.

Usually, Ruby would have been down there with them, letting the music fill her mind, letting it carry her worries and stress away on a tide of incredible, electric vibes.

But tonight, she felt off.

All the ice had melted in her gin and tonic, leaving some room-temperature water and a lonely lemon slice, but the money to buy another one wasn't in her budget. She had a food shop to do tomorrow, and Christmas was fast approaching.

The thought of seeing her mum and grandma smiling on Christmas morning was enough to lift her mood a little. Setting her glass down, Ruby turned to talk to her bandmates, who were sitting nearby.

'Did anyone ever find out what happened?' Clark was saying. They were talking about the gig they'd played the day before.

Trudy shook her head, the corners of her mouth turned down. 'No. But when I went to try and fix it, I saw that the plug had been pulled out of the wall.' She shrugged. 'Maybe someone tripped.'

It was a simple and likely explanation. But a strange feeling was tugging at Ruby insistently, the same one that had followed her since that day she'd been interviewed, and nearly crushed under a falling lamp. The feeling was like a shadowy figure tapping her on the shoulder, whispering in her ear: *No such thing as coincidence.* As she swirled the leftover tonic around her warm glass, another memory surfaced. When she was younger, she'd owned a battered edition of Sherlock Holmes stories. The concept of a detective had enthralled her, the idea that a person could tell so many things about other people from tiny clues often missed by an untrained eye felt like a superpower, and Ruby wanted it. To be the kind of person who could solve any crime using just their wits – well, she'd have gotten to the bottom of what happened at the gig in seconds. And maybe she wouldn't have needed a TV show to help find her parents…

Ruby, get a grip, she told herself. There was no use at all thinking like this. Nothing strange was going on and there was no explanation needed for why she was having so many accidents lately – she was just clumsy, that was all.

Clark, Trudy and Jim chatted away, raising their voices to be heard above the music. But Ruby didn't feel like talking much – it was just one of those nights. There was too much on her mind, and she still couldn't stop thinking about her interview with Davina. Every time her phone buzzed with a notification, she would whip it out of her pocket, hands trembling, convinced it would be someone from the show calling with bad news. She didn't even dare think about how she would feel if it was any other kind of news. The thought of a stranger ringing to say, *Ruby, we've found your parents…* was enough to send her into a cold sweat. It would change everything.

Soon enough, Ruby started thinking about saying her goodbyes, and going home. She was about to stand up, when she saw him.

Through the bodies on the dancefloor, through the dry ice that drifted across the room like smoke, through the flashing lights and the intermittent darkness. The glint of an eye in the flashing light. The corner of a smile.

A man, dancing.

His form seemed to reflect and absorb the blue and purple lights of the club, like a galaxy lived on his skin. Like *he* was a galaxy. Ruby could see electric blue undertones in his buzzcut, like the sheen of a raven's feather as he turned round and round, arms in the air, as though daring the stars to dance with him, too, and possibly succeeding. *And his clothes…!* Ruby stared, mesmerised, as his kilt fanned out around him like the tail feathers of a bird, his sleeveless orange vest revealing strong arms, the muscles gliding under the skin as he threw his arms up in the air, and danced, and danced, and danced.

Ruby smiled. The man's joy was transforming him into something radiant. Turning the dark club, with its sticky floors and dingy corners, into the kind of place where magic happened. As she watched him, she felt all her worries disappear too, for a moment, like a door in the universe had been opened right in front of her eyes, taking her breath away.

Unable to tear her eyes away, she reached for her drink. To her horror, her knuckles knocked against the glass. She turned away from the dancefloor just for a moment, as, almost in slow motion, she saw the glass slide across the table and begin to fall. *No, no, no—!*

A hand reached out and caught it. Ruby looked up.

It was him. *The dancing man.*

'Careful,' he said.

Ruby stared at him, stunned. 'Thank you,' she blurted out. 'But. You were just over there—'

The man pulled a black wallet from somewhere and flicked it open in front of her face. 'Health and Safety. Gin and Tonic Division.' He winked so quickly she almost missed it, and then the paper was gone, the wallet snapping shut. 'Can I ask, do you get that a lot?'

Ruby stared back at him, dazed. There was something about him – his confidence, his dazzling smile and perfect teeth. He seemed… different to other people. More confident. But no, that wasn't all of it. 'Sorry?'

'Knocking things over? Does it happen a lot?'

'All the time,' she found herself confessing. 'I'm just… really clumsy.'

'No,' the man said, and for a moment his carefree face was solemn. 'You're not. It's worse than that.' His eyes seemed to search her face. Ruby had never been looked at like that before. Examined. She felt like an insect in amber.

Something changed in the man's expression. As though he had been looking for something in Ruby, but wasn't yet sure if he'd found it.

'Merry Christmas,' he said cheerily.

And then he was gone, disappeared into the crowds and the darkness and the strobing lights.

'What...?' Ruby's mind was struggling to process what had just happened. He'd moved so quickly. One minute he'd been dancing, *she'd seen him,* and the next...

I'm just really clumsy, she'd said. *No,* he had replied, his eyes meeting hers, and *seeing* her. *You're not, It's worse than that.* She was struck again by the image of him, skin shining, smiling, spinning round in his fanned-out kilt. So much joy, bursting out of him, owning the middle of the dancefloor. An urge struck her to run after him, out of the club and down the road, just to grab his arm and ask, *who are you?*

She sighed, setting down her glass on the table. Except, to her dismay, the table wasn't there any more – she saw it too late, half a metre to the left of where it had been a moment ago – as her glass fell from her hand and tumbled through the air, gin and tonic suspended in a tragic arc, before the base of it connected with the sticky concrete floor, and the whole thing shattered with a *smash* all over the floor. Clear liquid spilled across the floor, and in it, Ruby could see her warped reflection.

Chapter Five

On Christmastime evenings, there were few places more magical to walk through than London. The streets glimmered with recently fallen rain, turning pavements into blurry mirrors that reflected the Christmas lights strung from lampposts to buildings, from windows to doors. It was the time of year when magical things felt a little closer to the surface; fairy tales pressing their noses to the windows of our world.

It was also the time of year when department stores in the city centre liked to decorate themselves lavishly for the Christmas season. Shiny baubles the size of small asteroids hung from shop windows, and entire buildings were turned into advent calendars, or wrapped in ribbons like a present, complete with glittery bows.

Henrik's department store was the best decorated of them of all. Attached to the front of the shop, high up, for all to see, an enormous snowman peered out. Its currant eyes were the size of car tyres, its carrot nose as long as a grown man. Lights glowed from within it, mingling with the beams of the streetlights to illuminate the road below. The wind picked up, and the snowman swayed with the force of it, the steel screws that held it in place groaning ominously under its weight.

Below the snowman, a man stood, watching the road.

It wasn't entirely clear what he was looking at – or who. Until a group of girls appeared, hailing a cab. Cheeks flushed with the cold, heads thrown back in laughter, they were merry, holding on to each other as they cheerfully stopped the cab and began piling in.

'Honestly, Rubes,' one of them giggled, voice echoing down the street. 'It's like you've got a curse!'

'I know!' Ruby's voice rang out, lively and familiar to the man after their conversation in the nightclub. 'And then I lost that twenty quid! I swear, it's like the past three weeks, bad luck keeps on following me around. I broke that thing. I lost that job. My heel broke, and I fell over in front of that fit dentist…!'

Their voices faded as the doors to the cab slammed shut one by one, its glossy black exterior reflecting the Christmas lights, and the night sky.

The girls' cab began to pull away, trundling slowly off into the night. Before it could get far, the traffic light at the end of the road flashed amber, then red, and the cab came to a stop, the girls inside visible through the frosty glass, laughing and nodding, teasing each other, telling stories. Ruby said something, her blonde hair glowing like pale fire through the frosty glass, and the others all roared with laughter, the sound of it dull outside the cab where the man stood. But he barely heard them – his attention had been snatched away.

By a noise.

Snicker-snacker. Chitter-chatter.

A whisper. A sneering, snickering murmur that raised every single hair on the back of his neck, and set alarms ringing inside his skull.

Something is here. Something that isn't meant to be.

The man looked up.

Directly above the taxi waiting at the traffic lights, the giant head of the Henrik's snowman was *tilting*.

A horrible creaking sound ripped through the silence of the street, like a door in a horror movie, opening slowly to reveal a monster. For a moment the man was frozen as the snowman's head lurched forward as if pushed from behind. But that was impossible – there was nothing behind it except the wall. And wind alone couldn't do this, the snowman was far too heavy for that.

Something more powerful was at work.

The creaking sound of metal being stretched past its limits screeched louder, as the steel cables holding the snowman in place were stretched further and further, creaking closer to the point of no return. And still, there was no explanation for the swaying.

Except… there! He could see them now – thin, grey fingers fiddling with the huge screws that bolted the snowman in place, and there was that chatter, the sound of small voices, floating down from above.

Snicker-snacker-he-he-he!

The man looked at the taxi; inside, the girls were still laughing, completely oblivious to the huge snowman tilting over the road. He imagined the impact it would have if it crashed down on top of the vehicle…

Without hesitation, the man whipped a strange device from his pocket, and pointed it at the traffic light. Silver and purple flashed in the darkness, small lights on the device sparking to life as it whirred, power flowing through it. The red traffic light holding up the taxi flickered, and then, as though responding to the whirr and flash of the man's strange, alien-looking device, it burned green. The cab shot forward, the other cars beeping as the device threw the traffic light system out of sync. But the cab drove on, safe and unaware, the girls inside still laughing and oblivious.

Just in time.

With a *snap* that echoed around the street, the last cable holding the snowman's giant, spherical head to the front of the shop broke. Sparks showered down like meteors falling across the night sky, electrics buzzing and circuits breaking with a crackle as all the lights on the snowman went out.

And then the head rolled forward, and started to fall.

Unnoticed by the man, across the street, stood a young police officer. PC Harry McLellan had watched those girls hail the taxi, making sure from a distance that they got in without any trouble, and found himself thinking back to similar evenings with his own mates. All those Christmastime outings, bundled up against the cold. The laughs they'd had, the trouble they'd been in, the countless joke presents.

And now it might all be changing. His fingers toyed with the velvet box of the engagement ring he'd been carrying in his pocket all week. And with it, a new life coming into view, just around the corner. *Well, only if she says yes, that is.* He imagined, for the millionth time, presenting the ring to his girlfriend and her reacting in horror.

Then a loud noise jolted him out of his thoughts, and a more horrifying image chased imaginings away.

The gargantuan head of the snowman decoration on the front of Henrik's department store was jolting violently, as though it was about to…

Harry felt his heart lurch as he watched as the head detach from the glowing body with an echoing *SNAP*.

The huge white ball fell almost in slow motion, like a blimp dropping out of the sky.

It was going to land in the middle of the street!

Whipping his head around to check for anyone who might be in the danger zone, Harry saw a woman walking with a pram, about to cross the road, completely oblivious to the looming threat descending from above.

Before Harry could move, a man appeared, sprinting across the street, coat flying behind him as he ran, hands outstretched. 'No!' he shouted, loud voice startling the woman out of her thoughts. She gasped as she saw the danger falling from above, and stopped dead. Just in time.

WHUMP!

The man disappeared underneath the snowman's head, as though it had devoured him in one gulp.

The street was silent. Harry gaped, eyes transfixed on the snowman head. It had sounded awfully heavy when it had finally hit the ground.

Was there any chance the man had survived?

Was it possible he had rolled out of the way at the last second…?

He couldn't have. The street was empty. The man was nowhere to be seen. Which meant—

With a *pop*, the left eye of the snowman opened. For one strange second, Harry thought it might be winking.

But then the man who had saved the woman and her baby clambered out, unhurt and grinning like some old-timey comedian or stuntman, the kind that dived from diving boards into tiny glass boxes, or hung from high-up buildings, or sawed themselves in half in front of a live audience. The inside of the snowman must have been *hollow* – and from the right angle, its open neck really had swallowed him up, whole and uninjured.

'Are you all right?' asked the woman.

'A pram?' the man replied, gesturing at the one she was pushing. 'At midnight?'

She pulled a face. 'It's my shopping!' she said defensively, and went on her way, unfazed.

Coming back to his senses, Harry scrambled to action. Running over towards the man, he blurted out, 'Oh my god, sir, are you all right? Are you okay? I'm so sorry!'

'I'm fine,' the man replied, and he did seem calm – as though far stranger things had come his way than a giant snowman's head. 'I'm fine, I'm fine.'

Harry's mind was racing. He'd best call for an ambulance. Alert the owners of Henrik's. Get the facts together for his paperwork. 'I'll have to report this!' he announced.

'Okay,' the man said, as if used to answering questions for police reports. 'My name is the Doctor. Occupation: not a Doctor. Current status: just passing by. Employer: myself. Address: that blue box over there.'

'Oh…' Scrambling for a notebook, Harry tried to keep up with the man's rapid-fire answers to questions he hadn't even been asked yet. He looked down the road to where this man – 'the Doctor' as he called himself – was pointing. A few metres away, a tall blue wooden hut stood waiting. Harry recognised it from his police training – an old-fashioned police box!

'And if you don't mind,' said the Doctor, 'I just got *snowmanned*. I want to go home.'

The young policeman stared at the Doctor. *Erm, okay,* he thought. *But, I still have to follow procedure.* Finally locating his notebook, he followed behind the Doctor as he walked over to the blue box. 'Doctor, er, what would that last name be?'

'Just the Doctor,' came the reply. Then the Doctor paused, just in front of the box. He turned to look at Harry, calm, not a hair out of place. It was almost unnerving, how little he seemed to be bothered by the situation. In fact, he was smiling.

'She's going to say yes,' said the Doctor.

Harry blinked. 'Who is?'

'Your girlfriend. When you ask her to marry you on Christmas Day.'

What? Harry had been worrying about this for months, about picking the right day to ask, writing the speech he was going to say to her before he got down on one knee. 'Wait a minute…' He was so nervous, he'd not told a soul, not even his best mate. 'How d'you know that?'

'My sonic screwdriver just went ping.' The Doctor held up a strange-looking gadget, that looked like two chrome ovals welded together, interspersed with segments of blue and gold. Purple light flashed out of it, illuminating a disc of that same golden metal engraved with strange, circular symbols.

It didn't look like any tool Harry had ever seen. 'That's a screwdriver…?'

The Doctor nodded. 'Which is sonic. And that precise ping is detecting a two-carat diamond in your pocket, which says engagement ring. And I'm guessing she's a she because ninety-one per cent of men would not choose a diamond. And Christmas Day, obvious.'

Who is this guy? Harry thought, flabbergasted. 'How d'you know she'll say yes?'

'Sales start on Tuesday,' said the Doctor simply, 'but you couldn't wait. And that's why she loves you. Merry Christmas!' With that, he turned, and disappeared inside the box.

Moments later, the young officer felt the ground beneath his feet start to rumble, and then all around him was a roaring noise, rising and falling in volume, as if ancient gears were grinding against some invisible force.

Then the box began to fade from view. It seemed like a trick of the light at first, the way it slowly disappeared, going from solid, to translucent, to semi-solid and then…

With one last heave, the box vanished.

Harry stood for a moment, blinking at the space where the box, and the man who called himself the Doctor, had been moments before. It was impossible. It had to be *magic*, or something like it.

Despite the impossibility of what he'd seen – the sheer wonder of it – all he could really think about were the Doctor's words, his prediction. The image of his girlfriend saying no, or laughing in his face, vanished completely, along with his fears of how things would go with his mates. Jubilant, happiness fizzing through him like sherbet on his tongue on Christmas morning, Harry McLellan ripped the page out of his notepad and walked back down the street, a whole new life opening up.

'She says yes!'

Chapter Six

London, 24 December, 2023

An irritated voice echoed down the street: 'Well, it's not my fault!'

Ruby turned down her road, laden with heavy shopping bags. They'd been a nightmare to carry home on the bus – a proper workout. At least she'd picked her red jumper and tartan shorts to wear instead of her fleece-lined joggers and winter coat. She'd be *melting* in those.

'Listen here, sweetheart,' said a second voice. 'I'm not what you'd call decrepit! I do my calisthenics, I keep myself fit and able, *thank you very much*. I did a Fun Run last Easter in twenty-five minutes flat – blisters the size of apples and I kept going! But all the same, how am I supposed to get round that great big thing of a morning?'

As she got closer to her house, and the angry voices, Ruby realised there was something blocking the pavement. A strange blue box, sandwiched in-between the front gates of the houses and the cars parked by the kerb. Ruby huffed with annoyance as she was forced to turn sideways in order to squeeze past it. As she emerged from behind the strange box, she came face to face with the source of the irritated voices.

Mrs Flood and Abdul. Her neighbours. Of course. Those two were always at each other's throats, bickering like schoolchildren, and it seemed that not even the season of peace and goodwill could stop them.

'Merry Christmas!' Ruby said to both of them, plastering a smile on her face as she approached; hopefully the Christmas spirit emanating from Abdul's incredibly festive jumper would overtake them and they'd forget why they'd even started arguing in the first place.

Not likely, she thought.

'Merry Christmas, Rubes.' Mrs Flood smiled brightly at her, before turning back to scowl at Abdul. 'You seen what he's done? Don't know what he thinks he's playing at, putting that there!'

The strange box *was* large – twice as tall as Ruby at least. Its windows were arranged in squares, two on each side, divided into six panels each. A small lamp was attached to the top of it, and the words 'Police Public Call Box' were spelled out beneath it in old-fashioned lettering.

Vintage, Ruby thought. *I like it.* Though she did agree it had been placed a little inconveniently. In any case, she didn't think it was fair for Mrs Flood to accuse Abdul of being behind it.

Clearly, Abdul didn't either. He massaged his forehead. 'What on Earth makes you think it was me?'

Mrs Flood pointed in his face. 'You've never liked me, that's why. I've seen you looking!' She turned to Ruby, her scowl morphing back into a smile as she remembered something. 'Isn't it your birthday, love?'

Ah. Ruby was hoping Mrs Flood wouldn't remember. For some reason, people loved to talk about how odd and unusual it was for someone to have a Christmas Eve birthday. Soon enough, Mrs Flood would be saying, *Oh, I bet everyone tries to get away with giving you joint presents!*

'It is, yeah, I was a Christmas Eve baby.' She nodded at the blue box, trying to change the subject quickly. 'So... what is that thing?'

Mrs Flood sniffed. 'Police box. I haven't seen one on the streets of London for fifty years.' She turned away from it, crossing her arms, as though she found the sight of it offensive. 'And I don't want to see one now...'

Snicker-snacker. Ticker-tacker.

Observed by no one – not Ruby, not Abdul, nor even Mrs Flood – a small grey hand reached from some hidden place, and sliced one sharp nail silently across the bottom of Ruby's shopping bags.

With a low ripping sound, the bottom of the bag began to tear. Before the first piece of shopping could slip through, the hand and the creature it belonged to had vanished, leaving barely a flash in the corner of the eye, as good as invisible.

Snicker-snacker. He-he-he.

Completely oblivious, Ruby shrugged in defeat at her neighbours' bickering. The police box was the least of her concerns; her shopping bag had started to sag while they were talking, and her shoulder hurt. The warmth she'd generated struggling off the bus with all her shopping had dissipated into the freezing cold December day, and all she wanted was to stomp up the stairs to the flat, take off her shoes, put on her slippers and drink a nice hot cup of tea. 'Well, season of goodwill and all that.' She smiled. 'Er, anyway, try not to kill each other.'

Turning quickly before either could ensnare her in another dispute, she walked up the steps.

Almost immediately, Ruby's shopping bag split open. Apples bounced down the steps, bruising and splitting. Packets of ham slid down the street, and, worst of all, a carton of eggs hit the floor with a definite *crack*.

'Oh!' Ruby exclaimed, frustrated beyond belief with all these accidents. 'I have had *enough!*'

As she gathered everything up, the thought of climbing to her grandmother's attic flat, staggering up a flight of about a million stairs with two armfuls of broken eggs and bruised apples felt like something out of a nightmare. She'd barely had time to go to the shops in the first place; it felt like one disaster after another these days.

Even on Christmas Eve!

Ruby opened the front door, pushing her way inside the building. *Honestly,* she thought, as she trudged grumpily up the winding stairs, *it's these constant accidents that are becoming the real nightmare.*

'It's me!' Ruby called out, as she turned her key in the lock and pushed open the front door, turning right and walking into the kitchen of their attic flat. Warm lights greeted her, emanating from the strings of fairy lights lining the long hall that led to the bedrooms – one for each of the women who lived there, three generations under one roof. 'I've got most of it. Except I dropped the eggs, which is obviously a massive problem cos the shops are closed for all of one day.' She could hear Carla bustling around somewhere in the kitchen, and her grandmother Cherry, calling for a cup of tea. The warm smell of ginger tea and bay leaves surrounded her like a hug.

Ruby set the shopping down on the kitchen counter just as Carla stepped out of her bedroom doorway, grinning. The orange and emerald headscarf she'd tied over her hair complemented her cardigan nicely, the mixture of cool and warm tones bringing the warmth and glow out in her complexion.

Something in her expression made Ruby pause. Carla's eyes were comically wide, her lips pursed shut in a smile, and her hands were vibrating with excitement at her sides.

Oh no. Ruby recognised that look. Carla had *news*.

'Guess what?' she burst out, before Ruby even had a chance to ask her what it was. 'We're having a *baby*!'

'No way!' Ruby nearly dropped the shopping she had begun to unpack. 'You're kidding?'

'A little girl!'

Ruby looked past Carla to the ladder and the half-empty can of paint still out from their efforts at redecorating. They'd have to tidy up quick. If it was another foster baby, they'd only have a few days until the social worker dropped the little one off at the flat. 'Seriously?'

'Isn't it brilliant?' Carla beamed. 'All of a rush, I couldn't say no.'

Ruby's mind was racing, half consumed with excitement and half with practicalities. *There'll be loads to do…* she thought as she opened the fridge and put the milk inside. Closing it, she smiled fondly at the photographs that covered every inch of the front of it. Wide eyes and toothy grins. Postcards and Polaroids, mementos and memories of all the kids that had passed through the house. All the children who had had a home here, however briefly. There was Matt, moved into his first flat, holding the 'M' mug Carla had painted for him, Divya in her cap and gown at graduation, Molly in Shanghai with her girlfriend during their travels. And so many others. Some had scrawled notes, or sent letters, everyone's different handwriting and fridge-magnet souvenirs and bright smiles decorating the fridge like a collage made out of different lives. All the lives that Carla had touched, all the children she'd fostered – some for days, some for longer. None quite as long as Ruby, though, who she had adopted.

And now there'd be another. A little baby girl, who would have a warm home to stay in all because of Carla. A rush of fondness filled Ruby's chest. Carla with her wide-open soul, and her hero's heart. Carla, who fought for the kids left behind by the system, who loved them like her own. And at Christmas too!

'Wait,' Ruby said, her mum's words catching up with her, filtering through the excitement. 'What do you mean a rush?'

'The baby's coming *today*.' Carla clapped her hands together, practically levitating with delight. 'Christmas Eve! Just like you, Ruby!'

'Oh *my*, that's amazing. How old?'

Carla's eyes shone. 'Newborn.'

'No way! Now that's a coincidence,' Ruby said, smiling.

The last of the shopping finally put away, and two eggs salvaged from the ruined carton, Ruby stuffed the shopping bags into a tote that Carla affectionately called 'our bag of bags' and grabbed the magazine she had bought for her grandmother, Cherry, before walking into the hallway.

'Coincidence is what I said,' Carla responded from the kitchen. 'Anyway, the social worker is coming round with the baby. She's on her way right now, actually.'

Wow, right now. This is really happening, Ruby thought as she ducked into one of the rooms off the long hallway, and walked towards the bed her grandmother Cherry was lying in. She was often tucked up under her duvet, especially on cold days, when she didn't feel like being up and about, but not even the grey winter days could dim Cherry's shine, or her fierceness, so she lay in bed playing games on her tablet, pretending she was reading the news, enjoying the warmth and rest.

'Good afternoon, Gran,' Ruby said, handing her a magazine. Cherry was like an old, benevolent goddess – she subsisted off devotion, prayers, and most important of all: offerings of magazines and cups of sweet tea. 'We're having a baby!'

Her grandma kissed her teeth. '*Mscheww*, that's Christmas ruined.' Cherry liked to play the crochety old lady, stuck in her ways. But Ruby knew she'd love the baby more than any of them. 'Sleepless nights,' Cherry elaborated. 'Stinking nappies.' Ruby laughed and kissed her grandma on the cheek. Cherry smiled at her. 'Ruby, baby, make me a cuppa tea.'

'All right, two ticks!' Ruby popped out of Cherry's room and went into Carla's.

Her mum was attempting to put together a jumbled pile of wooden beams that vaguely resembled the base of a cot... *if* Ruby turned her head at a forty-degree angle.

Carla's voice was slightly out of breath. 'It's been years since we fostered one this young. I can't remember how to put this thing together.' With a huff, she extricated herself from the mess of the cot, sitting back on her heels as she did so.

Ruby knelt down next to her; the carpet soft under her tights. *Is this what Carla did before she fostered* me? she thought. *Spent hours trying to put up a cot so I could be as comfortable as possible?*

Not for the first time that day, she found herself nearly overcome with emotion. The thought of a tiny little girl sleeping next to Carla's bed in a cot, giggling at the breakfast table, and splashing around in the bath was so sweet she almost felt like she'd eaten one of her grandmother's favourite boiled sugar lollies.

'A baby on Christmas Eve,' she murmured. 'Just like me.'

Carla smiled softly, giving Ruby all her attention. 'I got lucky, all those years ago. You know, Ruby, if you ever find her, your other mother, I'm going to tell her…' She broke off, her voice choked with emotion.

Ruby looked up. Tears glimmered in Carla's eyes.

'You were so *small*,' Carla said.

'Hey,' Ruby whispered. 'Come here.'

She wrapped her arms around Carla, patting her on the back. She never felt so safe as she did in her mum's embrace. And yeah, maybe Carla hadn't given birth to her, but she'd dropped Ruby off on her first day at nursery, and kissed every scraped knee before putting plasters over them. She'd read Ruby her bedtime stories, and given her the last biscuit in the tin more times than Ruby could count. She made the best ginger tea, and the best brown-stew chicken, and she gave the best hugs.

Everything Ruby knew about kindness and compassion she'd learned from the woman sniffling in her arms.

'I was lucky with my name,' Ruby said, trying to make Carla laugh. 'I bet this one's all Christmassy. Like Noelle. Or Eve.'

'Or Holly,' Carla giggled.

'Or *Carol*.'

'She's called Lulubelle!'

They'd finished putting the cot up just as the doorbell rang. The social worker for this case, Ruth Lyons, had bustled in, her cheeks flushed from the winter air, carrying the baby, who was bundled up against the cold and clipped securely into a car seat. They all stood around the kitchen table, cooing at the bundle of blankets.

'Oh,' Carla said, tickling the baby's chin. 'Lulubelle. What a terrible name.'

Ruby smiled, but Ruth didn't respond immediately, too busy setting the car seat on the kitchen table, along with a bag of baby food, nappies, and other newborn-related provisions. Not that Carla would have noticed in any case. Her hands were clasped in front of her chest now, and her eyes were basically big red hearts beating out of her face. She was already in love, cooing softly.

'What an *absolutely* terrible name!' Carla murmured again.

'Isn't it awful?' Ruth said fondly, handing a manila envelope of papers to Ruby. 'These can go in the Safe Box. Oh, happy birthday, Carla told me!' She put a big bag on the table. 'I raided the provisions from the office, but the cupboard was nearly bare.'

Carla scooped up the baby. Lulubelle's little fists waved in the air, tiny curls of black hair escaping her pale pink bonnet.

'So, it's a Section 20,' Ruth explained as they walked toward Carla's room, which was to double as a nursery. 'We'd have kept little Lulubelle on the ward, but we haven't got the staff.'

'What's wrong with the mum?'

'Just can't cope, poor thing. And the whole family is too complicated for words. But I'm hopeful.' Ruth smiled warmly at Carla and Ruby. 'I think she'll be with you for five or six days, till we can see what's what.' Her foot bumped into a half-empty can of paint that Ruby hadn't had time to tidy away just yet. 'Oh! I see you've been painting.'

Carla nodded. 'Making the place our own.' She nodded towards Cherry's room. 'Lord knows we are never going to move my mum, so we thought we'd add that special Carla and Ruby touch.'

Cherry's keen ears missed nothing. She shouted out of her door, 'I'm not going anywhere! Shackle me to dis bed, ya hear? And where's my cup of tea?'

Ruth hid a smile behind her other envelope of documents. 'Merry Christmas, Cherry! We should really get you a ground floor flat.'

Cherry's reply left no room for negotiation. 'Not. Moving!'

Meanwhile, Carla was taking Lulubelle out of her car seat, getting her comfortable in her new cot. Ruby watched her tuck the baby in with a little blanket. 'Here you are, Lulubelle,' she whispered. 'You're in with me.' A giggle. 'It's a terrible name!'

'I call her Lulu, that's not too bad,' Ruth said. 'Now, we're all off till the 27th but, maybe, as a rough plan, you could bring her to the hospital on Thursday? The 28th? Maybe ten o'clock? I'll text you. Just for a meeting with Mum, start bonding.'

Ruby had been looking through the bag of provisions. 'We need to go shopping first,' she said. 'These nappies are for six months old.'

Ruth groaned. 'Oh! I'm an idiot.'

But Carla seemed undismayed. 'Shops are still open, hold on…' She pulled a Polaroid camera out of her cardigan pocket. 'I like to take a snap,' she explained. 'Every little blessing.'

Pointing at the old-fashioned camera, Ruth asked, 'Can you still get film for those?'

'Course you can. You wait long enough, they're fashionable again.' She beamed at Lulubelle. 'Smile!'

SNAP!

A few minutes later, Ruby watched as Carla stuck the new Polaroid print on the fridge, between Molly and Divya. Some of the other kids were grown up now, and Carla had put their baby photos next to ones of their grown-up selves.

It's like time travel, Ruby always thought.

Or magic.

'There you go,' Carla said. 'Welcome to the family, Lulu. Lulu sounds nice!'

Ruby crossed to the hall and shucked on her coat, ready to go shopping once more. 'Okay, I won't be long, I can get some more eggs. Anything else?'

'No, I'll go,' said Carla, grabbing her coat and keys. 'I'll walk to Portobello Road and have a proper shop.'

'I can do it,' Ruby protested.

'No, but I can buy something for Lulu. It's Christmas and a birthday for her, just like you.'

Ruby smiled. 'You soft thing. She might only be with us a couple of days.'

'Yeah. But she's still family.' Zipping up her coat, she nodded to Ruth. The two women headed out the front door.

'I'm going out, Mum,' Carla called out to Cherry. 'Back in an hour.'

'Where is my blasted tea?' Cherry replied.

Oops! Ruby thought. 'I'll make it now!' she called back.

'I'm leaving you in charge, Ruby.' Carla said, barely visible as she closed the door behind her. 'Rule number one, *don't lose the baby!'*

Chapter Seven

Ruby leant against the kitchen countertop, desperately needing a moment to herself. *What an absolutely insane morning*, she thought, and a soft smile spread across her face. Despite the hectic turn of events, another baby, another tiny addition to their little family, was like a Christmas present come early. And on Christmas Eve too, just like her...

With a piercing trill, her phone rang, its chimes piercing the brief moment of quiet, vibrations shaking her pocket as she rummaged around for it. She answered on the fourth ring.

A voice, familiar from the television, and an interview which felt like lifetimes ago, said, 'Hi, is that Ruby? It's Davina here, Davina McCall.'

Ruby's heart stopped. *My parents.* In all the time she'd been waiting for news, trying not to hope too hard that the crew from the show would have found something – anything at all – about her parents, she hadn't let herself think about the impossible, but as soon as she heard Davina's voice, it was the only thing in her mind. *She's found my birth parents.*

'Oh my god. Hello!' Ruby took a deep breath. 'Um. Merry Christmas. It's nice to hear from you.'

'Look, it's not the best timing,' came the response, slightly crackly over the phone's speaker. Davina's voice sounded slightly apprehensive.

Ruby's heart dropped.

'And it's not good news. I'm sorry. I know it's your birthday, but… there's no trace of your mum or dad.'

Ruby barely heard her apologise. There was a dull roaring noise in her ears, as though she could actually hear the blood rushing through her body, up to her face. Her eyes pricked, and Davina's soft breaths through the phone sounded far away, muffled. Combined with the pressure behind Ruby's eyes, it almost felt like she was trying to hear Davina speaking from underneath the water of a swimming pool. The room in front of her went blurry, the fridge and its photos turning indistinct, the windows becoming nothing more than glowing squares of light.

'Ruby, I'm really sorry,' Davina was saying. 'We did warn you. It happens sometimes.'

Ruby swallowed hard, and said quietly, 'No, that's fine.' Blinking rapidly, she tried to clear the tears from her vision. Her throat ached. 'Of course. I… Thanks.' She couldn't remember the last time she'd felt such a blow. But even as she felt sad, she felt guilty too, for being so upset in the first place.

She had a family anyway. Carla and Cherry, and all the other kids.

But I wanted to know where I came from, she thought. *Why they gave me up.*

Ruby wanted to yell with frustration, to sink down to the kitchen floor and let the tears fall, to hang up without saying goodbye. 'Can't you keep looking?'

There was a pause on the other end. Ruby picked up the baby monitor to distract herself, fiddling with the buttons and turning it on. For just a second, she thought she heard a strange, oddly familiar noise.

Snicker-snacker.

Davina's soft, sympathetic voice crackled back through the phone. 'There's nothing more we can do. If your parents aren't on any sort of database ... we can't find them.'

No trace. Nothing.

Ruby shook her head. 'Okay, but isn't that unusual though? Not a single trace anywhere? In the whole wide world? Like, my mother's never left a blood sample, or – or *anything*?'

'I'm sorry, Ruby.'

'Okay. No, it's okay. Sorry. I get it.' Carla's voice echoed through her mind. *Manners, my love.* Ruby cleared her throat. 'Honestly, it's really kind of you to phone me yourself. Thank you.'

Ruby saw the baby monitor flash, indicating a sound in the room where Lulubelle slept. She frowned, and was about to hang up to go and investigate, but then Davina spoke again:

'There's something else I wanted to ask, actually.'

Ruby turned her attention back to the voice on the phone.

'Ruby, have you been having any, er, bad luck recently?'

She frowned. Davina's voice had taken on a strange quality. She sounded almost … scared.

'What do you mean?' said Ruby.

'Bad. Luck,' Davina whispered, a slightly manic note to her voice. 'Because ever since that day, it's never stopped.' Lowering her voice, she went on. 'I've been hit, I've been thrown, I've been bumped. I fell off a boat, *on dry land!* I've had accidents and collisions and I got trampled by a moose …'

Snicker-snacker. Chitter-chatter.
Don't let them see.

In the plush, beige-toned lobby of the hospital where Davina was taking this call – miles away from where Ruby stood in the kitchen of the flat – a small grey hand slithered out of the shadows.

Unseen by the nurses, or the manicured-looking receptionist of the hospital, or even Davina herself, it curled knobby fingers around the base of the Christmas tree. They were the same grey hands that had moved the coffee cup during Ruby's interview. The same grey hands that had ripped her shopping bag, and moved the table in the night club.

Not invisible, just unseen.

Lurking on the periphery, causing chaos.

'… And I can't help but think,' Davina continued, 'all these accidents, all this totally terrible luck … it all comes back to when I met *you*, Ruby. Those falling lamps were just the beginning …'

* * *

Still unnoticed by Davina, the leathery grey hand currently wrapped around the base of the enormous Christmas tree tightened its grip, and began to unscrew it.

Snicker-snacker. Ticker-tacker.

Back in the kitchen of the flat, Ruby's mind was racing, memories triggered by Davina's words. 'The funny thing is,' she said slowly, 'I actually *have* been having bad luck. I keep dropping things. Or – or tables aren't where they should be, or my shopping bag breaks.' There was a small gasp from the other end of the phone line. 'But,' Ruby stammered, 'they're just accidents. Aren't they?'

Davina's voice was panicky. 'How do we stop them? I am *begging* you, tell me how to make it stop, because I – I am *terrified*.'

Ruby felt a cold shiver of fear crawl over her skin. Davina hadn't answered her question.

'I—' Ruby started.

But Davina cut her off. 'Sooner or later, there's going to be an accident I can't avoid.'

'And next time,' Davina went on, from the hospital, 'it might be…'

She trailed off as she saw something from the corner of her eye.

There was a giant Christmas tree standing next to her in the reception of the fancy hospital, adorned with tinsel and giant glass baubles. As she watched, her mouth open in disbelief, the tree's huge branches swayed, as if a gust of wind was shaking it.

And then it began to fall.

Fear paralysed Davina. She couldn't run if she'd wanted to – her leg was broken from one of the million accidents that had plagued her since that interview with Ruby.

Pine needles bristled as the tree toppled over, baubles raining down like shiny spheres of death. And crowning it all, the razor-sharp points of the star that gleamed at its apex, shining like glittery knives, was falling straight towards her head –

'AAAAAGGHHHHH!'

Davina dropped the phone.

Chapter Eight

The phone line went dead. Ruby stared at her handset, puzzled. Davina's phone had fallen to the floor, that much was obvious from the clatter.

But had Davina just… screamed?

Shaking her head, Ruby set the phone down. Any other day, she'd be dwelling on Davina's strange questions, the accidents that sounded so similar to her own. But, despite the way the call had ended, all she could think about was the way she'd felt the moment Davina had told her that the search for one of Ruby's relatives had been totally unsuccessful.

Not a single relation.

No mum, no dad.

Not even an uncle or an aunt…

Tears pricked behind Ruby's eyes. She was glad there was no one else in the room – her face would have been splotched with red from holding back tears.

There's nothing more we can do, Davina had said. *We can't find them.*

Not a single trace.

A small sob escaped Ruby, lonely in the silence of the flat. However childish it was, a part of her had hoped for a Christmas miracle. Or even a birthday wish come true.

'Talk about bad luck,' she whispered to herself, and the sound of her own voice, thick with tears was enough to snap her out of it. 'Come on, Ruby. Pull yourself together.'

She looked around the flat – the Christmas lights that Carla had put up. The special glass for Cherry's sherry. The cards lined up on the windowsill. The baby monitor on the table, so she could hear everything going on in Lulubelle's room while she napped.

What a beautiful addition to their little family that baby was!

She's just like me, nineteen years ago, thought Ruby. Even if Lulubelle was only here for a day, Ruby would make sure she felt properly loved. *I'll put all my energy into her, all my focus.*

Christmas was no time to be sad. Not when she had such wonderful people to spend it with.

She wiped her eyes, and was about to put the kettle on for Cherry's tea when the baby monitor lit up again. At first, only a quiet whispering crackled through the speakers – like the window had cracked open and a breeze had come into the room.

Then she heard it.

Snicker-snacker-ticker-tacker.

She froze. From where she stood, there was a clear view down the hall. There was no one in the baby's room. The only people at home were her and Cherry, who was still in her bed.

The monitor crackled again.

Hicka-hacka-ha-ha-happy-birthday!

What?

Adrenalin pounded through Ruby, like electricity in her blood. The cup she was holding clattered onto the kitchen counter as she dropped it, and sprinted down the hallway, her boots thudding into the carpet. Anxiety twisted her stomach into knots. *What is that noise?*

She burst into the Carla's room and ran to the cot. Dread washed over her like a bucket of ice-water dumped over her head.

This can't be happening.

Lulubelle was gone.

Desperately, she cast her eyes around the room. Maybe Lulu had just crawled out of the cot. Stranger things had surely happened. *Right?*

Ruby dropped to her hands and knees, frantically searching under low cabinets and Carla's bookshelves. Nothing.

Except – *there!* A Polaroid print on the floor.

Ruby snatched it up, and nearly screamed. In the picture, a monstrous eye stared back at her – an eye surrounded by slimy, leathery-looking grey skin. She covered her mouth with her hand. The picture was still developing. Which meant that it had been taken recently. As in, *within-the-last-minute recently.*

Whatever creature it was the camera had captured… it was still nearby.

'Waaah!' A piercing noise from outside. A wail. No – a cry. 'Waaaaaah!'

A baby's cry.

Ruby looked up, just in time to see the edge of Lulubelle's blanket disappear through the skylight, whipped away from outside. As though pulled by someone. Or something.

The roof.

Carla's words echoed through her mind: *Don't lose the baby.*

Ruby didn't think, she just acted. Grabbing the stepladder they had been using to paint, she hauled it over to the skylight, and clambered up it, thankful for her sturdy black boots. She would find whoever had taken Lulubelle and stomp them to *pieces.*

Wind rushed all around her as she stepped onto the roof. Above her, clouds covered the blue sky with dark grey.

'Lulu!' she called, spinning around and around, desperate. And then.

Then.

She saw them. The grey shapes from the corner of her vision. The creatures with the horrible eyes from the Polaroid picture.

They were small, maybe waist height, with grey skin that gleamed like a toad's and the bulging eyes to match. Pointed ears stuck out from their heads, swivelling around like antennae. Where their noses should have been, two slits opened and closed, sniffing the air, smelling Ruby's fear. Thin mouths concealed rows of jagged, shark-like teeth.

The creatures were dressed in clothes that were almost nautical, that wouldn't have looked out of place on a pirate ship; striped trousers with patches on both knees, billowing shirts that were once white, reduced to dirty grey tatters that showed the creatures' thin ribs through the holes. One wore gold earrings, another a ragged and threadbare bandanna. To Ruby's total horror, the creature standing closest had a *Santa hat* covering their slimy bald head.

And worst of all, gripped in their horrible grey hands, was baby Lulubelle.

Ruby went on staring. 'What the hell…?'

'*Hissssss!*' One of the creatures bared its teeth, shaking its head menacingly.

Anger sparked inside Ruby's chest. 'Did you just *hiss* at me?' she shouted, walking closer. 'Was that a *hiss*? Oh, I have had enough of this. Let me tell you a thing or two—' She broke off. The edge of the roof stretched before her, and after it was empty space. The ground was several storeys below, cars the size of her fist, people small as insects. Wind whipped past her, throwing her hair into her face.

Ruby gulped. It would be a long way to fall, if she tried to fight these things for Lulu.

How do you fight a knee-height, slimy, pointy-toothed creature anyway?

'Oh god, I'm on the roof.' Vertigo made Ruby's head swim. But she couldn't let fear overcome her, not when Lulu was in danger. She turned back to them. 'Let me say, I'm *not* being hissed at, mate. And one more thing. *Give me back my baby!*'

But the creature only raised its head to the sky and called out.

Before Ruby could move, a rope ladder unfurled from the sky, dropping right into the air above the roof. She looked up. In the sky above the flat, dense black clouds had gathered, crackling with the energy of an approaching storm. They formed in a nearly perfect circle overhead. Everywhere else, the clouds were a normal, wintertime-afternoon grey, calm and peaceful. The storm had gathered only where these strange, baby-stealing creatures were.

She looked back down. Quick as lightning, the creatures had chucked Lulubelle's basket onto a hook attached to a rope that led all the way into the clouds. The basket was whisked upwards, swaying horribly in the wind, Lulubelle's terrified cries receding into the sky. The horrid creatures were going to drop her fifty metres if they weren't careful! They shot Ruby one last look with their bulging eyes, before they raced up the ladder, nimble and light on their feet, like ants swarming up the stem of a leaf.

'Where are you going?' she shouted. 'Where are you taking Lulu?'

There was no response. The creatures disappeared into the clouds.

Ruby had no choice. Fear thudded through her, but she pushed it down. Bracing herself, she ran to the edge of the roof and jumped.

The rope ladder swung wildly under her weight; she was much bigger than they were. Landing a few rungs up, she began to haul herself skyward, hand over hand, foot over foot. Vertigo gripped her throat, the floor underneath her was already getting further away. Wind pushed her this way and that. Her hands sweated.

And then the rope ladder started to *move*.

The last thing Ruby saw before she squeezed her eyes closed, were the roofs of houses, moving swiftly below her, as she was dragged over London by whatever was attached to the other end of the rope ladder.

Chapter Nine

Ruby clung on for dear life. The ladder was moving quickly, soaring over all the houses on her street, the ground rushing past beneath her. She could see the local park and the tower blocks in the distance.

What if I fall, she thought, *what if I lose my grip and—*

'Hey!' yelled a familiar voice. 'What the hell are you doing?'

Ruby opened her eyes. *Who is that?*

Running alongside the rope ladder, coat billowing in the wind as he leapt from roof to roof to keep up with her, was the man from the nightclub.

The Dancing Man, Ruby thought. *What is he doing here?*

'I'm just—' she tried to shout back but the wind snatched her words away. She was fifteen metres in the air, for crying out loud! And even if she could've been heard, how do you succinctly explain to a relative stranger that the incredibly cute baby your mum is fostering – the baby left in your care – has now been stolen by creatures from a fairy tale?

'What have you done that for?' the man yelled, as he jumped from a roof crowded with potted plants, to the edge of the next. His long brown coat caught the wind, fanning out behind him, so that it looked, for just a moment, like he was flying. 'Who sees a ladder fall out of a cloud and just... pops on?' He cackled. 'A ladder in the sky and you thought, "Yeah, I'll give that a go, babes!"'

'They've got the baby!' Ruby bellowed back.

The man jumped across another roof. 'Well,' he yelled, and Ruby thought for a second that he smiled. 'I haven't got any choice now!'

And, with a great running leap, he launched himself off the side of the nearest roof, arms outstretched, graceful and strong. He collided with the ladder, wrapped his arms around it and hauled himself up.

Ruby and the dancing man clung to the ladder. The streets of London flew past beneath them, trees and houses and traffic a blur, people with their dogs on afternoon walks, and the sparkling river Thames rushing past. Postboxes, pubs, foxes tipping over bins... all flying away into the distance.

She focused on his face. This man really did have the most extraordinary face, she thought. His smooth skin and easy smile made him young, but there was something glimmering in his brown eyes, something old and wise. Something that had seen to the heart of things – that knew the world already, that knew what made it turn. But above all those contradictions, his face was kind, she decided. Definitely kind.

I think I can trust him.

'What's your name?' the man asked her.

'Ruby,' she replied, shouting a little still over the howl of the wind. 'Ruby Sunday.'

'Hello, Ruby Sunday.' White teeth flashed in a boyish grin. 'It's a Sunday right now. That's a coincidence.'

Yeah, Ruby thought. *Been a few of those today.*

The man nodded at her. 'I'm the Doctor.'

Speaking of coincidence. 'I've met you before,' she said.

'Yep!'

'And now there are creatures, and they've stolen Lulu—'

'Goblins.' The Doctor nodded knowledgably.

'Goblins.' Ruby repeated, dumbfounded. The shock was nearly enough to distract her from the burning sensation spreading all over her sweaty palms. The rope was too painful to keep hold of. The effort it took to hold her own bodyweight on the rope for such a long time was too much. Her muscles burned with the effort.

'I can't hold on,' she gasped.

'Oh! Right, right, right. Wait. Wait!' The Doctor removed one of his hands from the ladder and plunged it into his pocket. 'I spend a lot of time hanging off things. So I invented these.'

From his pocket he pulled some black and gold fabric.

Ruby realised what they were. 'Gloves?'

'Intelligent gloves! Here, one each, put it on, quick.'

Ruby managed to detach one hand long enough for the Doctor to put a glove on her. Gold wiring stretched down each finger.

'Cos I thought, what's the problem with hanging on? The weight and the friction and the burn. So I got rid of 'em! The glove's a kind of super-kinetic-transfer of mass... well, look, it's like this.'

He grabbed the ladder. Ruby, whose arm was nearly numb with effort and pain, wrenched hers up to follow him.

Relief flooded her. Immediately, she was nearly weightless – as though all the strength it took to hold herself up had been taken on by the glove. *It* was lifting *her*.

'I'm lightweight,' she breathed.

The Doctor nodded, grinning. 'All the mass and density and mavity exist in the glove, not in you!'

Ruby opened her mouth to reply, but before she could speak, the rope ladder jerked and rippled underneath them and then began to rise, as though a giant had reached through the clouds and started pulling them upwards.

They both clung on, exchanging glances. Ruby was terrified, but the Doctor seemed strangely calm. Curious more than horrified.

'Interesting. They're pulling us in,' he said, in the same way someone might say, *Interesting. I never knew that octopuses have nine brains.*

Ruby said, 'But where? What's up there?' In the same way someone – probably Carla – might say, *HOW ON EARTH DID YOU LOSE MY BRAND NEW BABY?*

'The Goblins are up there,' the Doctor replied simply. 'And d'y'know why they're called Goblins? Because they gobble you up. And this lot want to gobble up the baby!'

They were high in the clouds now, the misty water vapour dampening their clothes and skin. It was getting colder too. Ruby remembered watching a documentary about planes once; the camera had zoomed in on the window, and she'd seen ice crystals on it. At high enough altitudes, water froze. *What about people?* she wondered. *Will we freeze to death on this rope?*

She wanted to ask the Doctor, but his attention was focused on the sky. That's how he saw it before she did.

'And this,' he said quietly, '*this* is where they feast.' A huge shadow fell over them. 'The Goblin ship.'

Ruby looked up. Above their heads, the round, bloated wooden keel of a boat blotted out the sun. It appeared to be made of gnarled, brown tree limbs – all twisted together in an intricate pattern to form a boat-shaped structure – that seemed to be pulsing with some strange life force. As if the wood woven together to make the ship was... still alive. As they drew closer, Ruby saw the sails were not sails at all, or even oars as they might appear, but *wings*, huge soaring wings that whispered as they captured the wind and used it to fly; wings made of sturdy, flapping leather, and something silky, like gossamer, or the fine silk spun by spiders. Portholes flashed in the last of the day's light, as they were lifted up, so close Ruby could have reached out to touch the bottom of this impossible flying pirate ship. She saw that the whole thing was held together not with nails, or human carpentry, but bound with ropes, and fastened with wispy grey threads that looked like cobwebs.

'It's beautiful,' breathed the Doctor.

As he spoke, a trapdoor became visible through the murk of the clouds. A yawning black hole through which the end of the rope ladder disappeared.

'They're bringing us on board.' Ruby looked at the

Doctor, trying not to let her fear show on her face. 'What will they do to us?'

'Oh,' said the Doctor absentmindedly. 'They'll eat us too, of course.'

And then darkness was closing over their heads, a rank, muggy warmth choking the air, making it harder to breathe, as they entered the belly of the Goblin ship.

The Goblins were waiting for them. As Ruby and the Doctor rose into the ship, they were greeted by a hundred pairs of bulging eyes, staring hungrily at them out of the gloom of the ship. Shafts of sunlight pierced the hull of the boat like knives, illuminating the hissing creatures that surrounded them. Hundreds of Goblins, some of them still winding the winch that had pulled the rope ladder back into the ship. One of the Goblins sniffed Ruby, and she could actually see it drooling with anticipation, already imagining how succulent the first bite of her flesh would taste. Her last thought before a sack was shoved over her head and she was dragged away by what felt like a hundred Goblin hands, was of baby Lulubelle. What if she was already Goblin tea?

And what if I'm next?

Chapter Ten

'I can't believe this.' Ruby struggled against the impossibly intricately knotted ropes that bound her hands to the mast pole behind her. 'I can't believe a single thing that's happening! *And*... it's my birthday!'

She and the Doctor were in a tiny room. The ceiling was at Goblin height, so their heads brushed it, even sitting down.

'It's your what-now?' said the Doctor.

Ruby huffed. 'Never mind me, they're going to eat Lulubelle! What time do Goblins eat dinner?' She yanked at the ropes again. But it was impossible: the Goblins had her tied up like a suckling pig ready for roasting.

The Doctor was tied to the other side of the big wooden pole, and she could feel his hands wriggling and searching, his fingers testing the rope. She hoped he was having more luck than she was.

'So, do I have this right, it's your birthday *and* Lulubelle's?' the Doctor said. 'Brilliant name by the way, I wish I was called Lulubelle. But back to the topic at hand. Two girls, both born on Christmas Eve...'

'Yeah, but that doesn't mean anything,' Ruby said. 'Seven billion people in the world, some of us have got to be born on the same day. It's just a coincidence.'

Ruby felt the Doctor pause in his escape attempt. 'Learn the language! Coincidence is what makes the baby *tasty*. That's how Goblins work, Ruby. Chance and coincidence and luck. That's how I spotted you, you've been having lots –' he lowered his voice to a whisper, as though he were about to say something he shouldn't – 'lots of bad luck, yes?'

'Yeah, but that goes way back. Lulu only arrived today. I started having accidents weeks ago.'

'That was paving the way. These Goblins are Time Riders. They can surf the waves of Time. They saw the chance of coincidence, so they went back, and wove you in.'

Surf the waves of Time? Ruby thought. *What is he talking about it?* 'So they…' A prickle of dread crept up her spine. 'Do you mean that it's these Goblins who have been causing my accidents?'

She twisted her neck, trying to see the Doctor's face. A small part of her hoped he was joking, or that this was all some warped nightmare. But the wooden floor underneath her felt so real, and she could see the motes of dust floating in the sunbeams streaming in through the wooden slats of the boat's hull. Even the air felt thinner, harder to breathe. She knew that was what happened at high altitudes – the air began to contain less oxygen.

'Were they trying to…' Ruby swallowed. 'To kill me?'

'No,' the Doctor said thoughtfully.

How can he be so calm? Ruby wondered. He was acting as though getting trapped in a strange ship with no way out, no plan and no idea where he was headed was a weekly occurrence for him. She watched as he tried to articulate why the Goblins had been causing her so many accidents.

'No, it's more like, if you walk through a day without any bad luck, then fine, that day's nothing. But if you have lots of accidents, that stitches you in, it weaves you into the day, you become all complicated and knotted and vivid.' Ruby had managed to turn her body so that she could see the side of his face. His eyes were lit up with excitement. 'All of it leading to a baby on Christmas Eve, same birthday as you, with a bedroom that's high in the sky, all convenient for a Goblin ship.' A smile had taken over his face – his whole expression lit up with discovery, like a scholar unearthing an ancient text they thought was lost for ever. Like a kid trying a new lolly.

'How do you know all this?'

'I don't!' There was that grin again. 'This is a whole new science for me, and I *love* it. The language of luck. It's brilliant. Because what's a coincidence, but a form of accident? Two things bumping together. Unexpectedly.' He turned to face her fully, and now the smile was directed at her. It was almost dazzling. 'Like you and me,' he said.

Ruby smiled back. This whole situation was bonkers, and she'd feared for her life more times in the last hour than she ever had before. But if she could have chosen anyone to be by her side, it would have been this strange man. The dancing Doctor, whose smile could light up the dingiest Goblin dungeon, who was exhilarated equally by danger and the pursuit of knowledge.

'Who are you?' she asked. 'How is it so easy for you to accept this, let alone be an expert on it? Time-travelling Goblins and all.'

The Doctor's eyebrows shot up. 'Oh! *Cha.* Hmph. No, just no. They're *not* time travellers. Excuse you. Time travellers are… great. Like, the best. Like. *Wow.* This lot, these Goblins just… bimble.'

Ruby resisted the urge to giggle, barely realising that he'd dodged her question about who he was. 'Okay, but if they're bimbling, why did they pick on Davina McCall?'

'Oh, well,' said the Doctor. 'That's just fun.' And with a flourish, he pulled both of his hands free from the ropes.

'How did you do that?'

The Doctor shook his hands, massaging them to get the blood circulation flowing again. A faraway look came into his eyes. 'Ah, well. I spent a long, hot summer with Harry Houdini.' A sigh. 'Now then.' He reached behind Ruby, his fingers digging into the ropes, performing a few deft movements before she felt the ropes fall away. Snatching her hands out of the loosened bindings, she cradled them to her chest. Her wrists felt sore and friction-burned, the skin rubbed raw.

The Doctor had already run to the door, trying to open it with no success. Now he was crouched, to avoid hitting his head on the low ceiling, rummaging through the pockets of his long brown coat. Eventually he pulled something out, something that sparkled dully – chrome and gold in the low light. He pressed a button on it and pointed it at the door. Nothing happened.

Ruby half-walked, half-crawled closer to get a better look. The device looked almost like a computer mouse without any wires – the edges curved, flowing into one another. Oval shaped and palm sized, with a few buttons, it was made of silver metal, interspersed with blue and gold sections, through which a bright light shone.

The Doctor pressed it and it buzzed, the light flickering. Still nothing happened.

The door remained locked.

'Wrong world,' the Doctor muttered.

'Why?' Ruby peered at the thing in his hand. 'What is that thing?'

'Sonic screwdriver. But a screwdriver needs screws. This lot bind everything with knots.' The sonic screwdriver disappeared back into his pocket. Ruby watched as he followed the ropes around the room like a sniffer dog, examining them, poking and prodding, muttering to himself and counting.

Ruby pushed against the door again but it was useless. 'We've got to get out. They could be eating the baby right now.'

The Doctor eyeballed a rope. 'What time were you born?' he asked, not taking his eyes off it.

'I don't know, they kind of guessed. Around two o'clock, I think. Two in the afternoon.'

The Doctor buzzed the sonic screwdriver at another bundle of ropes, and then looked at the device intensely. 'Right, so, language, tapestry, coincidence. That's the time for the feast. What time is it now?'

Ruby patted herself down, hoping her phone hadn't fallen to its death on the journey into the Goblin ship. It was still in her pocket. 'Five to two,' she read off the screen. Then, realising that mean they had five minutes until Lulubelle was getting dipped in Goblin ketchup and devoured, she said in horror, '*Oh no.*'

'Quickly, look outside,' the Doctor said.

Ruby ran to the wall, clearing a matted ball of spider's web out of the way so she could see down to the streets below. They were almost back in her neighbourhood. There was the corner shop, and the primary school a few streets over—

'We're circling back to your flat. The pattern is closing. We'd better hurry up.'

Ruby ran back to the door, throwing her whole bodyweight against it now, frantic with thoughts of Lulu being served up on a plate. 'Well, come and give me a hand, then!'

'I am learning,' said the Doctor, infuriatingly calm, 'the vocabulary of rope. This stuff is their version of wires and electricity, so if we trip the right switch…'

Without looking, he reached up above his head and grabbed a piece of rope, yanking it downwards. It pinged away when he released it and whipped through the room, slithering through the knots it had been tied into, whooshing past the windows and across the ceiling, until it shot right over Ruby's head, thudding towards the door, where it unravelled completely. There was a moment of silence.

Then the door fell open, revealing the hallway beyond. Ruby gasped. 'You can *speak rope*.'

The corridor was tiny. Cobwebs hung from the gnarled, rope-bound rafters of the boat, which let in golden streams of sunlight through gaps of varying sizes.

We must be above the storm clouds here, Ruby thought in wonder.

She was still barely able to compute that she was crawling through a Goblin-sized corridor, hundreds of metres in the air, with a man who had introduced himself only as the Doctor and could, apparently, speak rope.

'We can't exactly sneak around,' Ruby pointed out. 'We're like giants in this place.'

The Doctor looked around, pensive. 'Hm. I think even a leaky old Goblin ship has got the equivalent of…' He reached up, grabbing the frayed end of a rope that Ruby hadn't even noticed, half-concealed as it was in shadow, and tugged on it. A knot unspooled with a slithering sound and a trapdoor swung down in front of them, leading to a dark space in the ceiling of the corridor.

The Doctor grinned triumphantly. 'Ventilation shafts.'

Ruby followed him into the dark of the ceiling.

She'd seen scenes like this in movies – spies in black catsuits crawling determinedly through shiny metal spaces, watching people through grates in the wall, before dropping down through the ceiling, landing in a perfect pose and destroying the bad guys with a cutting one-liner and some perfectly executed mixed martial arts moves.

From the comfort of the sofa, munching on some popcorn (salt for Carla, sweet for Cherry), it was fun and exciting. Exhilarating, sure, but not too scary because she knew the good guys would win in the end.

But as she crawled through the claustrophobic, musty-smelling darkness of the Goblin ship, trying not to get booted in the face by the Doctor, her only ally up here (though she didn't actually *know* him), racing against time to save Lulu from being eaten by a horde of hissing Goblins, she wondered if the good guys ever won in real life.

The events of the past few years flooded through her mind – the hard times that she and Carla had faced, Cherry bedbound and confined to a tiny attic flat she could only afford because rent was kept low by the law. Davina McCall ringing her to say that they hadn't been able to find her parents. And now, Lulubelle, abducted and taken aboard a Goblin ship… her only hope of a saviour being Ruby – a 19-year-old girl who didn't even know who she was, or what she wanted from life, who still jumped on her bed with music blasting when no one was home, and wore short skirts in December because they frankly looked *great* on her, even if she did get a bit cold. She was responsible because she'd had to be, had to grow up young to deal with the cards life had dealt her, but she still felt like a kid sometimes.

Just a kid waiting for her life to begin.

In the dark of the Goblin ship, Ruby thought, *Maybe this is it. My life, finally starting.*

'That noise,' the Doctor whispered. 'What is that noise?'

Ruby blinked, jolted out of her own thoughts. Now that he pointed it out, there was a sound: a low, beating sound, steadily growing louder.

It sounded like… 'Drums,' Ruby said. She checked the time. 'Doctor, there's only three minutes until two o'clock.'

'It's the dinner gong,' he replied. A shiver ran across Ruby's skin. 'Must be.'

In front of them, a large gap in the ventilation shaft beamed light into the dark tunnel. Frantically, they crawled over to it, hoping they would see something that could help them figure out where Lulubelle was.

What Ruby saw through the gap she would never forget for as long as she lived.

Below them, was a dining hall. Hundreds of Goblins gathered around a long table. It was almost like a family Christmas gathering, if the family members were all two feet tall, dressed in piratical rags and thirsty for the blood of children. At the end of the huge, wooden room, a heavy pair of canvas curtains hung, as though concealing something.

'Look! There she is,' the Doctor whispered.

Ruby squinted. *He was right.*

There was baby Lulubelle, swaddled in her blanket, now in a Goblin-made basket of wood rope, presented like some kind of sacrifice. She gurgled, completely oblivious to her fate, and the Goblin crowd roared in jubilation, as loud as a ten-foot wave crashing on the shore, ready for the feast.

The creatures stomped their feet, the whole ship reverberating with the savage rhythm, like a galley full of soldiers sailing off to war. They cried out and clapped their hands, until the war chants started to almost resemble… a song.

Ruby was about to climb down there herself, snatch Lulubelle up and fight the whole ship of Goblins, when a reedy voice cried out, '*Hit it!*' and raucous, skull-shattering music suddenly filled the hall.

An elevated stage lit up, light shining from sconces shaped like scallop shells and, to Ruby's disbelief, a Goblin band was revealed, heads bowed, instruments at the ready. *Entertainment for the feast*, she realised.

The crowd erupted in even louder screams, as the Goblin band began to play.

We've got a baby, we can feast!
We can dine three days at least.
Baby blood, and baby bones,
Baby butter for the baby scones.

Spotlights swung, highlighting each member of the cacophonous band. A Goblin drummer smashed out a fierce rhythm on a drumkit made of hollow tree stumps, headbanging next to the Goblin marimba player, who produced resonant chimes with every tap. There was a Goblin blowing a conch shell, who stood opposite the Goblin guitarist, fingers a blur over the strings on their tree-branch guitar, as they sang ad-libs for the leading lady, a Goblin with masses of blonde curls, barely held back by a headband the same faded red as her tattered, medieval-style gown.

> Little baby feet, little baby toes,
> Ev'ry one of us wants the nose!
> Baby's had such very bad luck,
> Now into baby, we will tuck!
> Eat the baby, add some salt!
> Bay leaves, barley, powdered malt!

To Ruby's horror, a Goblin in a chef's hat scattered salt and pepper, bay leaves, and powdered garlic all over Lulubelle, even crumbling some gravy granules over her nose.

'They're seasoning her!' Ruby exclaimed.

'Amazing,' murmured the Doctor.

'No, it is not!' Ruby's angry whisper was almost lost in the sound of the Goblin song reaching its crescendo. A Goblin in an eyepatch darted forward and tried to lick some of the salt off Lulubelle's cheek, but the other Goblins roared and pulled them back, hissing and narrowing their eyes. Ruby felt cold all over. If that Goblin wasn't allowed to eat Lulubelle… then surely none of the others were allowed either.

What were they all waiting for? Or *who*?

All the Goblins turned towards the end of the room, where the huge curtains made of canvas and leather hung ominously at the far end of the dining table. The drumbeats got louder, and the lead singer tossed her curly hair and sang:

> *Now baby's salted, she's a treat,*
> *Her destiny – it's time to eat!*

With a great grinding groan, the dining table began to *move*. The black tablecloth wasn't a tablecloth at all, Ruby realised.

'It's a conveyor belt,' the Doctor said. 'But where's it going?'

Lulubelle giggled, her crinkly newborn eyes still closed. The conveyor belt rumbled along, wheels turning, carrying the baby closer and closer to the looming curtains. *What could possibly be behind them? A huge oven? A pot of boiling water? A meat grinder?*

The Goblins were all singing louder now, a rasping, raving chorus of voices like a monstrous choir, some of them even dancing the jig in their pirate boots, their bulging eyes nearly popping out of their heads with excitement.

> *Baby we need!*
> *Baby we feed!*
> *Eat with our teeth!*
> *Better than beef!*

Cold sweat was dripping down Ruby's back. *I have to do something!*

'Doctor,' she started, and then broke off.

The Doctor's face was twisted with fear – no, with realisation. 'Oh no,' he murmured. 'Oh *no*.'

At the far end of the room, the curtain was lifting.

'What is it?' Ruby was frantic. 'What's behind the curtain, Doctor?'

But all he said was, 'I wondered whose ship this was.'

They didn't have to wait long to find out.

Behind the curtain writhed a mass of grey, slimy flesh. Like a huge slug, the biggest Goblin that Ruby had seen so far lurked at the end of the table, expanding and deflating as it heaved breaths in and out through flaring slits in its nose. Its body was formless, its distorted face monstrous and enormous, the distance from its chin to its forehead longer than Ruby herself.

Two dark, glittering eyes, each as big as Ruby's head, stared out at the Goblin hordes who worshipped it.

Worst of all was the mouth.

Right at the end of the conveyor belt was the creature's huge, gaping maw. A wet, red tongue licked non-existent lips, leaving a slimy saliva trail that glistened as the creatures opened its mouth in anticipation, revealing row upon row of those shark-like teeth, serrated and sharp enough to bite through steel, filling the pit of its mouth like bone-yellow knife-points.

The conveyor belt was going to drag Lulubelle right to where this Goblin giant was sitting.

On stage, the conch-playing Goblin launched into a wild, brassy number, and the whole room went wild.

He's the Goblin King, yes, the Goblin King,
He's not a myth, he's an actual thing!

The band continued to sing, while Ruby and the Doctor looked on, aghast. Well, Ruby was aghast – the Doctor looked like he'd just unwrapped a puppy on Christmas morning. There's was a hint of horror in his expression though. Maybe an incredibly vicious puppy. With fleas.

And we love his chin, when it's wobbling!
He likes to dine on coincidence,
It fills him, builds him up, and hence!
He! Can! EAT!

A Goblin with darkly glittering eyes sang, 'Five hundred puppies with golden fur!'

'Orphan boys with jet black hair!' another joined in.

'Circus clowns with a red balloon!'

From somewhere below, Ruby heard a Goblin say to their friend: 'He can eat me, he makes me swoon!'

Yuck! thought Ruby. To her, this Goblin King was the ugliest thing in the world, especially since he was about to eat the baby left in her care. But to the Goblins, this massive creature must be beautiful and mesmerising, meant to be served and worshipped. He was like their rockstar god, and they'd done all this baby-stealing trickery just to feed him. To keep him happy.

Lulubelle was only metres away from his massive mouth, drawing ever nearer.

Ruby knew that she had to do something now, or the baby would be lost for ever.

'STOP!' she screamed, slamming her fists against the floor. 'You leave her alone! *Leave her alone.*' But her shouts were drowned out by the macabre Goblin music. For a moment, it sounded like a funeral song. 'Doctor, help me. What do we do?'

The Doctor was scanning the walls with his eyes and hands, yanking a piece of rope here, undoing a knot there. 'Hold on!' With a great heave, he ripped away a piece of timber, scattering cobwebs and splinters of wood. In the gap behind the wood was a massive knot, rope twisting in on itself like a bundle of pale snakes.

The Doctor reached inside and *pulled.*

The knot sprang undone, a hundred pieces of rope uncoiling all at once, whipping through the room as they untangled and came loose. The trapdoor under their feet gave way, and Ruby barely had time to scream, before they were falling, tumbling through the air right into the middle of the Goblin feast below.

Chapter Eleven

Ruby shielded her face as the conveyor belt rushed up to meet them. The dimensions of the Goblin ship were so small that it wasn't a very long fall – like tipping off the top bunk of a bunk-bed – but her shoulder burned with pain as she collided with the ground. Springing to their feet, Ruby and the Doctor looked around.

The Goblins were silent, staring in confusion at the two humans who should have been locked up in the ship's dungeon.

'Right, so,' the Doctor said awkwardly. 'Tough crowd.' He looked towards the Goblin King, and gave a surprisingly graceful curtsey. As he did so, he reached over to Lulubelle's basket and grabbed it. Ruby snatched it off him with shaking hands and looked down to check on Lulubelle; the baby seemed unharmed, wriggling in her basket and staring up at Ruby with keen interest. Ruby was terrified, looking around at the salivating Goblins and their awful King, but the Doctor seemed strangely composed. 'Your Majesty. Hello. I'm curtseying. I'm also the Doctor. And, this is my friend, Ruby Sunday, and I'd just like to say that…'

There was a pause. *Oh, no, he's lost it,* Ruby thought. *They'll see that this is all just a distraction.*

But then the Doctor's face lit up, and he started to click his fingers, snapping them to a very familiar rhythm. 'You like songs, don't you?' Now his feet were tapping out the rhythm, that broad smile spreading over his face.

Despite herself, Ruby smiled too.

'I saw you!' the Doctor told the Goblins. 'I know you do. Who doesn't love a song? Giving rhythm to the world!' He shimmied. 'Am I right?'

To Ruby's utter shock and delight, the Goblins started nodding and clicking as well, stamping their feet. *Oh!* It was the same rhythm as the song from before. The Doctor had picked up the rhythm and the tempo, and it was so catchy she almost wanted to sing along. The Goblin crowd was positively jubilant.

A sharp elbow jabbed her in the ribcage. It belonged to the Doctor. 'Follow my lead,' he whispered out of the corner of his mouth. 'And don't let go of that baby.'

Ruby nodded, clutching Lulu's basket even tighter.

The Doctor turned towards the crowd, raising his voice to address the room. 'That's it! Clap for the funny man!' Clapping his hands together, he led them all. 'And you Ruby, clap, you're in a band! Come on!' Ruby had barely touched her hands together before the Doctor took front and centre stage. He pointed at the Goblin band, still standing stunned on stage, and yelled, 'Rock it, Janice!' Without hesitation, the Goblin band launched back into their lively number, and the Doctor burst into song. His voice was clear and loud, with a deep timbre. He was, Ruby thought, mouth hanging open, a natural born performer.

Cos the Goblin King, oh the Goblin King,
It's so good to meet you, you great big thing,
I can see you're having a fun day,
Meet my friend, she's Ruby Sunday!

'What?' she shrieked.

But the Doctor was already dragging her to the front of the table, pressing something into her shaking hands – it was one of the intelligent gloves! She slipped it onto her hand, as the Goblins cheered for the next verse.

The Goblin King stared at her expectantly with his wide, wet eyes.

Ruby gulped and launched into song herself, lyrics tumbling through her mind from a place of sheer desperation.

It's good to meet you, good to greet you,
Good to say, 'How diddly-deet you!'
It's my birthday, my oh my,
I'm fifty miles up in the sky!

The Doctor nodded at her, so she stared the Goblin King right in his terrible face and kept singing:

But Goblins, you can go to hell,
Cos you're not eating Lulubelle!

The Doctor's voice started again, loud and smooth-toned, as he took the stage for one last verse.

Me and Rubes, we got just one hope,
If I have understood that rope,
Cos stuck up there, when things got hot,
I think I found the Master Knot.
The Master Knot has been undone,
THAT's when we start having fun!

The Doctor looked up towards the ceiling, and Ruby followed his gaze. All over the gnarled wooden ceiling, ropes were suddenly flying around, timber and knotted cobwebs all coming undone, as the rope whipped through its fastenings.

The Master Knot! Ruby realised. *When we were trapped in the ceiling, and the Doctor pulled away the plank of wood and exposed that huge, secret tangle of ropes…* She knew that some houses had a master key, a key that could fit any lock. Open any door in case of an emergency. *Well,* she thought with grim satisfaction, *I think this qualifies as an emergency.*

The Goblins watched on in horror as the rope pinged around, faster and faster, whooshing back and forth over their heads as it unravelled like a loose thread on the hem of some trousers caught on a twig.

Ruby felt the Doctor shift his weight beside her, stabilising his centre of mavity, as though readying himself to move, quickly.

'Ruby,' he said out of the corner of his mouth. 'Hold on tight, yeah?'

'What are you—?' she started, but broke off. The Doctor's eyes were fixed on the roof, and the rope pinging from one end of the ship to the other, racing closer to where they stood, right in front of the Goblin King's gaping mouth.

The rope came swinging back down in their direction, and Ruby just about had time to hook Lulubelle's basket tighter around one arm and grab hold of the Doctor before he reached up with one hand and grabbed the rope, halting its progress completely. There was a deafening silence.

The Doctor smiled at Ruby, his eyes bright with intelligence and the thrill of adventure. She was reminded, inexplicably, of the first time she had seen him, dancing with wild abandon in the dark.

'If you reverse an intelligent glove,' the Doctor said, grinning, 'you get heavy.'

And then the gloves were glowing, bright light racing down the golden filaments woven into the fingers. And Ruby, clutching Lulubelle's basket so hard her knuckles were white, clung to the Doctor as he jumped off the dining table conveyor belt, taking her with him.

They smashed through the floor of the Goblin banquet hall, splinters and wood chips raining down behind them, Ruby's bright blonde hair blowing all over her face. The Doctor's long coat wrinkled in her hand as she clutched it, the back of it blowing upwards as they fell. The wood scratched her legs as they broke through the twisted hull of the flying ship like it was made of wet tissue paper, their weight augmented by the glove. In a flash, they had punched through it completely, bursting out into the cold winter air of the sky.

The roaring, devastated cry of the Goblin King was the only thing that followed them.

Chapter Twelve

They fell, hurtling through the sky, as the streets and blocks of flats of London rushed up to meet them. Ruby screamed, holding fast to Lulubelle's basket and to the Doctor; his arm was stretched over his head, clutching the rope in his intelligent glove.

Cold winter air blasted all around as Ruby, Lulubelle and the Doctor dropped further and further out of the clouds that hid the ship and closer to the pavement, hundreds of metres below.

Ruby's eyes watered. It was like falling from a plane without a parachute. Through her blurry vision, and the hair whipping in front of her face, she could just about make out the winding, alley-like street of Portobello Road, and Notting Hill Gate with its beeping taxis and double-decker buses and bustling pedestrians.

If I can see all these people, what happens if they look up? Ruby wondered. *Will they see me?* She almost didn't care – her only real concern was getting two feet back on the ground, and putting Lulubelle back in her cot where she belonged, safe and sound.

'How do we stop?' Ruby yelled; her mouth and cheeks were wobbled around by the rushing air so it came out more like *Blough do be bwop?*

'Love the glove, Ruby!' the Doctor replied, managing to be mysterious and mischievous whilst falling to certain doom.

'What?' Ruby was so scared, flying towards the ground, that she started praying for her life:

To whoever is listening! I know I've never spoken to you before, and I know I wrote an essay for RS in Year 9 about how you don't exist, but I'm, like, just a mortal girl, so what would I know? Also, this isn't just about me! It's about Lulubelle, too. She's so tiny, she hasn't even had a chance to properly live! She hasn't felt the sun on her face in summer, or eaten chocolate cake on her tenth birthday. And she definitely hasn't written any potentially blasphemous essays in RS, so you can't be mad at her for that. Plus, I'm really sorry. Just promise you won't let us get splattered to death—

A blinding light lit up the light blue sky. Ruby abandoned her attempt at a prayer and looked up. It was the glove, glowing even brighter.

The Doctor winked at her. 'Told you, love the glove!'

As soon as the glove started to blaze with light, Ruby felt herself begin to slow down. Her tartan shorts lifted up at the edges, making her think that the real divine intervention had been whatever voice told her to wear shorts and tights today instead of a skirt.

Past her boots, the roof of her own house was rushing up to meet her. She was gliding now, the cool air slipping past gently, a feeling of weightlessness spreading through her whole body. Her hair waved gently in front of her face, as though she were underwater. The rope stopped short, dangling them two feet above the flat grey roof of Ruby's house. The Doctor let go.

They had barely any distance left to fall. One heart-pounding second later, Ruby's boots thudded down, firmly back on the floor. *Or the roof, rather,* she supposed. Lulu's basket was a reassuring weight in her hand, grounding her. Peering inside, Ruby felt her whole body relax. Lulu's eyes were peacefully closed, her little hands curled into fists, her chin tucked into the pale blankets that swaddled her. Ruby brushed the bay leaves and garlic powder off her, bending down to place a kiss on her forehead.

'Well,' came the Doctor's voice. 'That was...'

Ruby straightened up, looking at him. 'Yeah. So. Um.'

A bright smile cracked over the Doctor's face, his eyes twinkling. *There it is again,* Ruby thought. He might look young, but there's wisdom there. *Or something. Like when I tell Cherry about something daft I did on the weekend, and she laughs because she was young once, and she knows why I did it. It's like that.*

She felt laughter bubbling up inside her. 'We did it!' she said, giggling, 'Oh my god, there were *Goblins.*'

The Doctor was laughing too now, a fantastic rumbly laugh, that was so full of *funniness* it made Ruby laugh even more. Her sides started hurting. The adrenalin of their flight was dissipating, but she felt like she could have vibrated out of her own skin with happiness and relief. Without thinking, Ruby wrapped her arms around the Doctor, hugging him. He laughed even louder, and hugged her right back. They'd done this *together.* Survived the belly of a Goblin ship, prevented Lulubelle from being devoured like a Christmas turkey and come up with a pretty decent musical number on the spot. Maybe they'd even thwarted Ruby's bad luck for good. And all in one afternoon. Ruby felt the Doctor squeeze tighter before letting her go. *We did it all by trusting each other.*

Ruby stepped back and looked out over London. Christmas lights were coming on, even though it was still completely light out, giving the whole city the look of a toyshop window, lit up for the Christmas season. The people on the street looked like windup soldiers, marching about their business beneath a blue sherbet sky, dotted with clouds of clotted cream. On an ordinary day, she would have said it looked magical, but really – *thankfully* – it just looked like everyday life. She'd seen crazier things now: flying pirate ships, and Master Knots; tiny, hissing Goblins and their gargantuan Kings. But Ruby herself felt very real – both boots on the ground (well, *roof*) again, Lulubelle's basket clutched in her hands.

She was home.

Chapter Thirteen

The flat was lovely and warm inside, Christmas lights still twinkling, and carols crackling through whole house, beaming out of Cherry's old radio like the audio equivalent of hot chocolate. She could smell the latest scented candle that Cherry had ordered online 'by accident'.

Ruby felt tears prick at her eyes. It felt so good to be back.

They had come back in through the skylight, the ladder still balancing where Ruby had left it, hours ago, when she propped it up so she could chase the Goblins onto the roof.

She jiggled the handle now, making absolute certain that the skylight was firmly locked shut, before slipping the sleeping baby out of the Goblin basket, and wrapping her in another warm blanket, cradling her to her chest.

'Who's that?' came Cherry's voice. 'Carla?'

'It's me, Ruby! I'm back. Sorry, I, erm, got a bit distracted—'

'Well, I've given up on that cuppa and opted for a life of abstinence!'

Ruby winced guiltily. The Doctor grinned at her, and walked to Cherry's room. 'Hi there,' he said. 'I'm the Doctor.'

Oh, he's a charmer, Ruby thought. She stifled a laugh. She could almost imagine Cherry looking him up and down.

The response was classic Cherry. 'The last doctor I saw tried to murder me. So you can stay away!'

'Oh, you don't need me anyway…'

Ruby saw him point to the shelf of family photos. She knew that wall like the back of her hand. There was one of Carla and Ruby packing up their Manchester flat, taken on self-timer. One of Ruby and Cherry watching soaps in bed in their PJs. And one from years and years ago, the whole family at the Christmas Market, a tiny Ruby in stripy stockings tugging Carla's hand towards a ride. Cherry's obstinate expression still made them all crack up years later. You could practically hear her voice through the photo saying, 'A *woman of my age and distinction… I am not going on* that!'

The Doctor beamed at Cherry as he finished his sentence: 'You've got your family looking after you.'

'Yes, I do.' Ruby could hear the pride in Cherry's voice. 'We three queens of the sky, up here in the attic.'

'And your name's Cherry?' the Doctor asked.

'It is.'

'Cherry… Sunday?' He sounded delighted.

'Like a tasty treat!'

The Doctor laughed. 'Nice to meet you, Cherry Sunday.'

'Lawks!' Cherry giggled. 'What a way him nice.'

Footsteps in the hallway signalled the Doctor's return to Carla's room. Ruby handed him the glove. He took it, putting it back in his pockets, which seemed endlessly deep. She suspected they were filled with surprising objects.

'Are we safe, then?' Ruby whispered. She'd been looking at the skylight. Past the glass, dark storm clouds still roiled in the sky above then, the storm hovering over Ruby's street. One thing was clear: the Goblins weren't gone. Far from it. It would be so easy for them to come back and find Lulubelle. They could send hundreds of Goblins this time. *Or the King himself.* She squeezed her eyes shut. 'What if that ship comes sailing down? What do we do then? Could they get their revenge? Take us back?'

The Doctor was looking out of the window. 'I don't think they invade,' he murmured. 'Their world is up there, and they creep into this one, on the edges.' He moved to step away from the window, but his foot caught on a wire trailing from a lamp. Ruby hadn't even seen it, but it was too late. The lamp tilted and fell, tugged by the wire. The Doctor darted forward and caught it just in time. Ruby's heart thudded in her chest. *Did the Goblins do that too?*

'Accidents!' the Doctor said. '*That's* how they get us.'

Ruby remembered Davina, as well as her own clumsiness. She'd hoped that taking Lulubelle back would cause the Goblins to lose interest in her. Hoped that maybe she'd stop being so clumsy and having such bad luck. But they hadn't gone anywhere, the storm clouds still hung there in the sky, the ship buried somewhere inside them, waiting for what? What if they took their revenge by making Ruby's life (and the lives of everyone around her) an accident-ridden misery?

Keeping her voice even, she tried not to let her panic bleed through. 'Do they cause *all* accidents?'

'Maybe.' This idea seemed to amaze the Doctor, as though their run-in with these tiny grey Goblin menaces were rewriting his understanding of the world. *But they couldn't be, could they?* Ruby thought. *How could those creatures cause all the misfortune in the world?* That didn't make sense, not the probability of it, not the science… Ruby's mouth turned down. *Nothing about today has made sense. So you can probably forget science and probability.*

The Doctor was bustling around the room now, checking for loose cables and sockets, testing the stability of the cot and running his hand down the wooden skirting board, checking for splinters. 'The trouble is,' he said, as he accident-proofed the room, 'the coincidence has bound Lulu to Christmas Eve. I could take her out of the day, but she's too connected. I think it would actually cause her pain. So, we're stuck, we've got to sit it out till midnight.'

Ruby frowned. Nothing that he'd just said made sense to her. 'What do you mean… "take her out of the day"?'

The Doctor paused, just for a moment, then kept checking the electrical outlets. 'Technical phrase.'

'Okay. What does "take her out of the day" mean *technically,* then?'

'It doesn't matter, because I can't do it.'

Ruby was getting frustrated now. She felt like a kid again, stuck in primary school, being spoken down to by a teacher who knew infinitely more than her and wouldn't explain a thing. 'But how would you *take her out of the day?*

Doctor, I still don't even know who you are. When we first met, you said you were Health and Safety. Is that even true?' She was breathing a little heavily. The whole day had been so *much*, and *confusing*, and now her one ally, the only person who knew what she had gone through, the only person she had thought she could trust with all of this, was being weird and secretive. 'And don't you dare say "Elf and Safety", because I am *not* in the mood for Christmas puns right now.'

The Doctor rummaged around in his pocket and pulled out the same wallet from before. He flicked it open to the pieces of paper in the middle. Before, they'd said *HEALTH AND SAFETY OFFICER*, with a government seal beneath and some random numbers. Now there were just five words.

Ruby blinked. 'That's not what it said before.'

'Well, what does it say now?'

'"I'm the Doctor",' Ruby read. '"Trust me".'

The Doctor grinned. 'It's psychic paper.'

'It's what?'

'The paper is psychic. Shows you whatever I want you to see.'

Ruby blinked, completely exasperated. 'What the *hell* does that mean?'

The Doctor looked up, eyes wide, his mind already somewhere else. 'Oh! Is there anything in the kitchen? Anything burning?'

Ruby gasped and ran for the kitchen, the Doctor on her heels. After the events of the today, she half-expected to see a tiny Goblin army, lighting torches on the hob and honing the blades of their pitchforks with the knife-sharpener.

They burst into the kitchen.

Nothing.

Ruby let her breath go, relieved, her heart still thudding in her chest. The Doctor moved past her, moving pans and the toaster, checking electrical sockets and inspecting appliances.

'Houses are death traps!' he said, picking up the kettle and turning it upside down. 'Check everything, the wiring, the plugs…' He trailed off, staring at something. Ruby followed his eyeline. The fridge. All the photos.

'Who are they?' he asked softly.

Ruby shrugged, smiling. 'That's the family. Carla's children. They're all the kids she's fostered over the years.' Just saying that word, *family,* made something warm and full of light swell in Ruby's chest. She was so full of pride, she almost didn't notice the expression on the Doctor's face. A tiny wrinkle formed between his eyebrows as they drew together. The glimmer in his eyes. Was it longing? Or intrigue?

'Wow,' he said, his voice full of soft wonder. 'So many.'

'I know. We're still in touch with some of them.' She smiled, remembering all the Christmas cards that had flooded in over the last few days, coming in response to the cards she'd helped send a few weeks ago. She and Carla had spent an afternoon writing messages and slipping boiled sweets into envelopes before lugging the bag to the local post office, each card bursting with red and green glitter and drawings of holly boughs and Christmas bells. 'Well, lots of them stay in touch, actually. Carla's amazing.'

That strange look hadn't disappeared from the Doctor's face. His intelligent eyes gleamed with uncertain emotion and, as he stood looking at the photographs, so still she couldn't tell if he even breathed, Ruby wondered, just for moment, if he hadn't transformed into a magnificent statue, right there in her kitchen.

'You've got the biggest family in the world,' he said at last.

'I have,' Ruby said gently. She couldn't have said why, but she knew it was imperative she be gentle to him, just then. 'What about you?'

There was a pause, and it seemed to contain a whole history inside it, a whole world of pain and unmanageable sorrow. 'I've got no one.'

Ruby opened her mouth to say something – anything to make him feel better – but then he had whirled round and was checking again for potential accidents.

'Make sure the oven's turned off!' he called, halfway down the hall already, as busy as could be, rattling the heaters, checking for loose batteries, knocking on doors to test their structural integrity, straightening picture frames on the wall, making sure no nails stuck out that someone could get snagged on.

Ruby blinked and kept checking things in the kitchen. She tidied away a few birthday cards, sent by her mates. There was a massive one from the band, with blurry snaps of her all over it, pulling some truly hideous faces. There was even the one Jim had taken after she'd shaved her whole eyebrow off by accident.

Reality seeped back into her awareness, seeing those cards. She had a life, a whole life that was not irrevocably changed by what had happened today. *Other creatures exist, and there are ships that fly, and languages made of knots and ropes instead of words. And a man, named the Doctor, who appeared right when I needed him.*

'If you told me I'd spend my birthday fighting magic,' Ruby said, 'I'd have called you daft.'

The Doctor's voice came from down the hall. 'It's not magic! It's a language. A different form of physics.'

'Yeah,' Ruby said. She knew that physics explained why massive metal planes could fly, and why the Earth always spun round the sun and didn't fly off into space. But it might as well have been an enchantment to her – she understood one just as little as the other. 'So, basically magic, then. But how? Where do these things come from?'

'There was… an incursion,' the Doctor said. His voice was quieter now. 'Into this world. D'you know the Giggle? When everyone went mad? That was caused by a Drastic Transgression known as the Toymaker. And he brought his legions with him. This is his legacy.' A pause, his voice growing quieter still, until Ruby couldn't tell if he was even talking to her; if she should even be listening. 'Forces of nature, but forces of a different nature, writing their own rules. So now I've got to no rules to follow, no rules to fall back on. And I am out of my depth.'

Cherry, who had clearly been listening to their entire conversation as they shouted back and forth down the hall, said, 'You're a crazy man.'

The Doctor laughed, his expression turning from stormy to light in a second. '*C'est moi, Cherie.*'

Ruby started to laugh with him, wanting to help dissolve the tension in the air created by the Doctor's quiet, worried tone, but she was cut short by a jangle outside the front door. Keys clanked in the lock. *Mum!* Ruby thought. *Act normal, act normal. If you don't give anything away, she'll never know what happened. Stay calm. Stay. Calm.*

The door swung open.

Chapter Fourteen

Ruby watched as Carla pushed the door shut behind her, shopping bags in both hands. 'Here comes Santa, laden with presents!' Carla announced, laughing. Then she stopped short, seeing the Doctor. 'Who's your friend?' she asked Ruby, her eyes never leaving his face.

'Um, this is … the Doctor.'

The Doctor smiled brightly. 'Hiya!'

If I'm going to surprise Carla with a stranger in the house, I'm glad he's at least a charming one, Ruby thought.

But Carla's face had gone a bit grey. She dropped the shopping. 'There's nothing wrong, is there? Is she all right? The baby?' Without waiting for an answer, she rushed down the hall, pushing past them where they stood at the doorway of her room.

'No,' Ruby babbled. 'No, she's *fine …*'

Carla shoulders sagged in relief as she saw Lulubelle, snug as a bug in her cot, wrapped up in blankets, her little face peeking out serenely from under her little cap. She stroked Lulu's cheek, and then turned round. 'It's not Mum, is it?' she asked, walking into Cherry's room.

That is just like Carla, Ruby thought. *Worried sick about everyone, giving them all the care and kindness she possibly can, without even taking a pause for breath.*

A pang of guilt went through Ruby. If Carla knew what they'd been through in the last few hours – if she knew what Lulubelle had been through – she'd probably pass out in a dead faint.

'What's going on?' she heard Carla ask Cherry, before repeating it in patois: 'Wah gwarn?'

Cherry huffed. 'I cyaant get a cup of tea roun' here fi love not money.'

Carla laughed. 'Mi get yaah packet of humbugs. Like Scrooge, 'tis the season.'

Ruby could hear Cherry's muttered thank yous, and the crunch and crackle of plastic wrappers as she opened her favourite Christmas treats. Cherry had once told Ruby that she used to buy Carla humbugs at Christmas after getting back from the hospital, where she worked as a midwife after arriving in the UK in the 1960s on a big ship, a passenger liner, all the way from Kingston, Jamaica. She'd met Desmond, the handsome, Blue Mountain-born tailor's apprentice – who would become her husband and Carla's father – in London a few years later, and the rest, as they say, was history.

For some reason, she remembered the phone call with Davina.

There's no trace of your mum or dad.

I'm really sorry.

Ugh. She'd have to tell Cherry and Carla at some point. They'd want to know. She knew they'd be nothing but supportive, and probably even upset on her behalf. But it still hurt a little.

Shaking her head, she tried to dispel the thoughts.

'So why do we need a doctor?' Carla was saying, having come back to stand by the cot. 'I hope my little chicken Lulubelle is all right!' she crooned in a baby voice.

'Routine visit,' the Doctor said. 'That's all.'

But Carla's attention had been snagged on something else. Bending down, she retrieved a piece of paper from the floor.

Ruby's heart stopped. *The Goblin picture. She's going to freak out. What can I tell her?*

Carla squinted at the image. 'What's that supposed to be?'

Ruby and the Doctor glanced at one another. 'Um,' Ruby stammered. 'I don't know.'

'Is that an eye?' Carla brought the photo up to her face. 'No!'

'It's a toy,' the Doctor interjected. 'It's the eye of a toy.'

'What toy?'

Ruby gulped. 'It's a toy that I... er, chucked out.'

Carla narrowed her eyes. 'She's too young for toys anyway. Where d'you get a toy from? You haven't left the house, have you? Or taken Lulu out in the cold?'

Ruby felt her throat tightening. She hated lying to Carla. What was she supposed to say? 'Yes, I mean no...' she stammered. 'It was just that – it wasn't... I didn't mean to...' To Ruby's horror, she felt all the emotion of the day hit her at once. 'Oh my god, Mum,' she blurted out. 'Can we just stop? Can we just stop all of this for a minute? Cos I've just – I've had enough. This has been the worst birthday ever.' Her voice cracked. 'It's Christmas, and my birthday, and it's a *disaster*.'

The Doctor's eyes widened. 'No, no. There was a problem, yes, but it's gone now, don't you think? No need to bother your mum with it, is there?'

Carla looked bewildered, worried and suspicious all at the same time. 'What sort of problem?'

The Doctor jumped in. 'It was nothing! And it's gone. It's really, *really*, gone. And before it was gone, it didn't even matter—'

But Ruby wasn't finished. This whole mad day was catching up with her, and despite the Goblins and the terrifying, heart-stopping minutes she'd spent flying through the air on a rope ladder and crawling through the belly of a magical ship, all she could think about right now was that phone call.

'They phoned me.' The words just came out. 'From the TV show, I mean. This afternoon, while you were out. Just before…' She cleared her throat. 'It was Davina McCall. She said they couldn't find anything. My mum or dad. No sisters or brothers or cousins, there was nothing.'

Carla eyes widened, her hands pressing against her heart. 'Oh, sweetheart.'

The Doctor fell silent. 'I didn't know.'

'I'm sorry darling. Come here.' Carla opened her arms, and Ruby stepped forward and practically fell into them, sniffling. 'Oh, Ruby.'

Carla's warm, strong arms encircled her, and in an instant, Ruby felt like a little girl again, running to her mum after school ended, being swept up in the best hug ever, Carla's perfume and the soft skin of her neck all adding up to a feeling like the perfect blanket of calm had settled over her.

'I'm glad you didn't find her,' Carla whispered fiercely. 'D'you hear me? Glad! Because I don't know if I could make room. You're all mine, that's what you are.' Ruby tried not to cry. There was so much love in her heart, it was in danger of spilling over. It was true that finding her parents might have helped her understand why they left her, but it wouldn't have helped her understand who she was. *This* was who she was. Right here, right now. Carla Sunday's daughter.

Ruby Sunday.

Maybe everything will be okay after all, she thought, the ball of anxiety in her chest finally releasing, unravelling just like the Master Knot had done. *As long as we have each other. As long we can give each other a hug at the end of long, scary day. If I can have that,* Ruby thought, *it doesn't matter what life throws at me, or that I don't quite know what I want to do with my life yet. I'll be all right. More than all right.*

I'll be happy.

Chapter Fifteen

The Doctor watched Carla and Ruby hug, watched Carla's fingers grip Ruby's shoulder, holding her close, and he felt at once terribly young and also ancient. The love they had for one another shone out of both them. He could almost see it – as bright and golden as a solar flare. They were at home in each other's arms.

Smiling softly, he remembered everyone who had been home to him over the years. Almost too many to count. Each one just as important as the other, each one so vital to this vast universe.

'Isn't she gorgeous?' Carla grinned, turning to the Doctor.

'Yes,' the Doctor replied, warmth spreading through him. 'She is.'

'I was thinking, you know…' Carla continued. She picked up Lulubelle's Polaroid print from her bedside table. 'When I was out. Counting, and calculating…' A soft, proud smile. 'Would you believe, Lulubelle's the thirty-third child I've fostered.' She held up the picture. 'I've got everyone's photo. Have a look, on the fridge, they're all there. I had some of them for days. Some for weeks, some for years. But only one of them stayed.' She turned back to Ruby. 'You made my life, Ruby. You can wonder about your parents, of course you can. But I wonder who I'd be, without you.'

The Doctor didn't know why he spoke. Sometimes, when he witnessed people like this, displaying this deep care for one another, it sort of … reflected back out of him. Like he was a mirror for other people's love. So he didn't really think before he spoke; the events of the past few hours replaced in his mind by the emotion of the moment. Ruby and Carla were so open, he wanted to open up, too.

'I'm adopted,' the Doctor said.

Ruby blinked. 'Are you?'

'Yeah,' he nodded slowly. 'Only found out recently.'

'That's a coincidence,' Carla said.

The Doctor shrugged. *It was, wasn't it?* Distantly, he heard Ruby's voice, whispering tersely, 'Don't say that!' But memories were taking over his mind, people and places he had been and loved. All of them, smiling in his mind.

Outside the window, the sky darkened.

'Do you know who your parents are?' Carla asked, not noticing.

'No,' the Doctor said. 'I was abandoned.'

'Doctor!' Ruby gasped.

'Oh!' Carla said, fussing with something by the cot, completely unaware of the effect her words were having. 'So you're a foundling, just like Ruby.'

The moment the Doctor realised what he'd said, a cold prickle slid down his spine. This was far too many coincidences. And coincidences were what the Goblins fed on, what sustained them, what they loved. They'd come swarming like ants to a sweet left on the road in summer. How could he have been so reckless and forgetful? Ruby was staring at him with wide eyes, fear visible in every aspect of her expression. No, no, no. When he'd seen her on the roof, when he'd jumped onto the Goblin's rope ladder, he'd only had one objective in mind. Protect her. And now he'd done the opposite.

A feeling was growing in the air. Something shadowy and alien. The Doctor risked a glance out of the window.

Carla kept tidying, shaking her head as she said, 'Can you *believe*? Three foundlings, all here, in one place, on Christmas Eve. I don't know if I've ever heard of a bigger coincidence!'

The words had scarcely left her lips when a huge *clap* of thunder split the air, like distant, planet-sized cymbals crashing together in the sky. The whole house shook.

Goblins.

Ruby and the Doctor ran to the window. The dark clouds were almost black now, moving as they watched, descending lower and lower, until they covered the roofs of the taller houses.

'Maybe we'd better not talk about coincidence, okay?' Ruby said, her voice shaking.

The Doctor approached Carla slowly. The Goblins were swarming now, and who knew what they had planned. They were a threat he had never encountered before, an entirely new realm of possible chaos and destruction. New ways for people to get hurt. Or even eaten. Not a single one of these thoughts did he let show on his face. Instead, he arranged his features into a mask of knowing calm. *I've got way too much practice helping other people stay calm whilst extraterrestrial, interdimensional threats descend upon the Earth.* 'Carla.' He smiled. 'My lovely, would you mind just putting that photo down…?'

But Carla clutched the picture of Lulubelle close and grinned at it, oblivious to the approaching threat. 'I took a photo of little lady Lu, soon as she arrived.' She was using the cutesy baby voice again and, despite the encroaching Goblin threat, Ruby looked absolutely mortified. 'Oh, look at her, though,' Carla continued. 'She's so gorgeous! Don't you just want *to eat her up?*'

'Oh, god,' the Doctor said under his breath. 'Now *that's* a coincidence.'

A gigantic rumble of thunder boomed out, drowning out his voice. It was a sound like the end of the world, like a thousand lions roaring. Once, on another planet, the Doctor had seen someone almost struck by lightning. They were standing in a field, dark clouds over head, when the air suddenly filled with static electricity, causing their hair to float in the air around them, flowing towards the sky like someone had turned off the planet's mavity or, at the very least, significantly reduced it. As the thunder rumbled overhead, the Doctor remembered the terrified look in that person's eyes, just before they had started to run. That same electric charge was in the air, now crackling over his skin, building and building until—

Blinding white light filled the room.

CRACK!

CRACK!
CRACK!

The window smashed, impacted by an unforeseen force. Glass rained down around them. Time seemed to slow down and speed up all at once. Next to him, Ruby yelled, flinging her hands up in front of her face.

He felt something then, though at the time he wasn't sure precisely what. Later, he would look back on this moment and understand. And the understanding would bring grief like a gut punch.

As the Doctor looked up, trying desperately to identify the source of the *cracking* sounds, the ceiling of the flat began to split in half. A dark void zig-zagged all the way across it, snaking out into the corridor and cracking the ceiling in two. Pieces of plaster fell around them, chips of paint flaking off and spiralling down onto the carpet. Wind howled through the window, rushing in through the jagged pieces of glass sticking out of the smashed window, and blowing through the house like a hurricane. Pieces of paper flew into the air, book pages flapping like the frantic wings of doves.

'What the hell?' Carla screamed over the howling wind.

'Don't move, don't move!' the Doctor shouted over the noise. 'Don't—' He froze. *No.* The crack wasn't just confined to Carla's room. It was *moving* – racing down the hallway like it had a mind of its own. A strange, volatile energy was emanating from it – something that raised the hairs on the back of the Doctor's neck. He'd seen cracks before, but this was different. The sight of *this* crack, this split, conjured to mind empty darkness, the feeling of something stolen, or missing. A violation, a wrongness. A loss.

He sprinted out of the room, chasing it as it snaked across the ceiling, cracking the roof of the flat, exposing wiring and red brick, crumbling chunks of plaster and yellow insulation.

The crack raced towards the kitchen and the Doctor followed it, ducking as it hurtled through the doorframe of the kitchen, splitting it in half. Woodchip rained down around his head.

He stood in the kitchen, breathing hard, staring upwards.

The crack was slowing down. A great jagged line had split the kitchen ceiling in two, but now the crack's progress was less rapid. It navigated its way to the light fixture, which swung violently before falling off in a shower of sparks. That seemed to halt its progress slightly. As the Doctor watched, it inched forward, growing thinner as it lost momentum, before slowing to a stop right before it reached the kitchen window.

Through that window, he watched as the dark clouds receded, fading into the distance like a fleet of ships, pale clouds settling in to fill the space. Normal sky was visible through the cloud cover, the colour of a winter afternoon.

Had they really retreated?

Perhaps the damage to the house was the entirety of their attack; one last retaliation as they realised the Doctor and Ruby had beaten them. The sky was definitely clear of

dark storm clouds now. It seemed the Goblins might be…
gone.

'Perhaps a piece of luck,' the Doctor murmured to
himself. 'At last.'

The crisis seemed to be averted. It was funny, though.
He'd been so certain the Goblins had been about to attack.
Why on Earth had they retreated without getting their
revenge? They didn't seem the types to settle for light
property destruction. Eating people was more their style.
And yet no one had been taken.

Well, no need to question it. Their departure was a weight
off his shoulders, and now he could leave in peace, safe in
the knowledge that he'd helped save Lulubelle just in time
for Christmas.

Not too shabby, Doctor, he thought. *Not too shabby at all.*

Turning around, he popped back down the hallway,
surveying the damage as he went. Wincing at the chunks
of ceiling plaster and hunks of wood that had fallen to the
floor. The air was thick with dust. And on the ceiling, the
crack was deep, jagged and dark, marring the once-cosy
look of the flat, and instead making it look like an explosive
had detonated somewhere nearby. It must have severed an
electrical cord, too. The whole flat looked darker than it
did before.

Colder.

Though maybe that was just the freezing cold December
air rushing in through the broken window.

Carla stood in the ruins of her room, the crack looming
above them, paint peeling off its edges.

'All good?' the Doctor asked, perhaps a tad too pleased with himself.

'What the hell was that?' Carla looked distraught. 'Look at the ceiling! And the window. It's the middle of winter, I'm going to freeze. Who's going to come out and fix that on Christmas Eve?'

The Doctor was barely listening. Out of the window, the last few dark clouds were rolling away. 'Bye-bye,' he said softly. 'Ta-ra!'

'Who are you talking to?' Carla asked.

'No one, nothing, just…' He stopped, his eye caught by a blank piece of paper. The Polaroid print. The square where the photo of the bulging Goblin eye should have been, was empty. Relief flooded through him.

They're really gone.

They'd done it – Ruby and he had done it. He looked at Carla, grinning properly now. The blankness of the Polaroid print proved it. Time had written the Goblins out of this story. They were gone for good.

'But…' Carla gestured to the smashed window pane. 'But the whole flat just cracked in half! Stop grinning and tell me what on Earth just happened!'

The Doctor was jubilant. 'Oh, don't worry about that!' He pointed out of the window at the cloudless sky and the cluster of skyscrapers on the horizon. 'See the UNIT tower? I've got friends in there. They can help with compensation. Ask for Shirley, she'll see to it that it's all fixed.'

'That's the Nitwit Tower,' Carla said in disgust. 'They're all outer-space nutters. Spending our bloody taxes on chasing monsters that don't exist. We haven't got monsters, we've got *subsidence*.'

The Doctor laughed. 'Okay, well, maybe we should sit down, and tell you a Christmas story, Carla. What d'you think, Ruby?' There was no reply. *She must have gone to sit with Cherry and calm her down.* 'Ruby?' he called out, louder this time.

No reply.

He popped his head out into the hallway. 'Ruby?' Turning back to Carla, he raised an eyebrow. 'Where did she go?' There was no response. A feeling of dread was settling over him. Above him, the crack loomed like a terrible shadow.

'Ruby?' He ran into Cherry's room, but she looked strange, staring blankly ahead, and did not acknowledge him. Ruby wasn't there.

He ran down the hallway. Maybe she'd left the house; maybe she'd needed some space. But the door was closed, her keys on a dish by the front door. Opening the door, he ran out, stopping short at the top of the stairs to listen for footsteps. There were none.

'Ruby!' he shouted. But the only reply he received was the sound of his own desperate voice, echoing around the empty space.

Ruby was nowhere to be found.

Chapter Sixteen

But Ruby was just here! the Doctor thought as he ran back to the flat. *She was right behind me. Wasn't she?*

The door to the flat swung open when he pushed on it, creaking loudly, like the door to a ghost house. When he stepped in, it was cold, in the way old buildings are in winter, if the heating's been off for a while. A permeating, enduring cold that seeps through stone walls and crawls under doorways. But it was also cold in a different way. The fairy lights were off, the music had died. Maybe the damage to the building had affected the flat's power.

Or maybe, said a small, scared voice in the Doctor's mind, *something is very, very wrong.*

Footsteps in the hall. The Doctor turned. 'Oh, Carla, it's you.' He gestured out to the hall. 'She wasn't there. Where's she gone?'

Carla just frowned at him. Above her, little flecks of plaster floated through the air, coming detached from the cracked ceiling. 'What are you on about?' she said. In her arms, she held Lulubelle. But… something was off. The Doctor peered at her. Carla wasn't wearing the bright headscarf from before. It was a dull grey, dour knitted one. In fact, all her clothes were dull. And her face… that was dull too. Her eyes were blank, uninterested in the baby that gurgled in her arms. The Doctor expected her to cuddle the little baby closer and start cooing and kissing her face, but Carla only rolled her eyes.

'I'm looking for your daughter,' the Doctor said slowly.

'Don't be daft,' Carla said. 'Lulu's not my daughter. I'm fostering her.' She shifted Lulu onto her hip, holding her without really *holding* her, as though she were just a sack of dirty clothes. 'Just for a couple of days.'

'No,' he said. 'I meant your daughter, Ruby.'

Carla looked at him like he'd grown a third head. There was no recognition in her eyes. None of her usual spark. No sign of the smile that usually appeared instantly when someone mentioned her daughter. 'Who's Ruby?'

The Doctor froze. *Oh, I was so wrong. The Goblins* did *attack.* 'Your daughter,' he tried one more time. 'Ruby.'

Carla rolled her eyes again. Before the crack, he had never seen her do that. She had seemed so kind. 'I told you,' she snapped. 'This is *Lulu*. And she's a right old pain.' Under her breath she added, 'Last thing I need. A baby on Christmas Eve.'

'But…' The Doctor's heart was pounding. *What have I done?*

Horrified, he ran right past Carla, down the hall, to Ruby's room. He burst in. Cobwebs hung from the ceiling. There was no bed, no bookshelf. No fluffy fairy lights, or keyboard, or the smell of Ruby's perfume. Instead, rickety shelves full of dusty knick-knacks filled the space. Cans of old paint clustered on the floor. A stepladder leant against a few cardboard boxes gathered in a dingy corner.

'Hey!' Carla called. 'What on Earth do you want in the spare room?'

But the Doctor barely heard her. His mind was racing with possibilities, each more awful than the last. Running back down the hall, he opened Cherry's door.

'Ruby?' he said breathlessly. 'Do you remember Ruby?'

The old lady looked smaller than he remembered. There were lines on her face that hadn't been there before – deep grooves between her furrowed eyebrows. Frown lines. The crow's feet she'd had before, the laugh lines, all the beautiful evidence of joy, all the mementos accumulated over of a lifetime of smiles were… gone. She looked defeated. Even her room was dark and cold. An old glass of water stood on the dusty bedside table. And there were no Christmas sweets to be seen. Her sparkle was gone. The twinkling in her eyes extinguished by something that looked a lot like loneliness. Despair.

'Do you…' The Doctor swallowed. 'Do you remember Ruby?'

Cherry sneered at him. It was an expression that didn't seem to fit her face. She was a wise and generous woman with a heart of gold; he'd been able to see that after spending only a few minutes in her company. It was as if that Cherry was gone and she'd been replaced by a robot.

'What are you talking about?' Cherry hissed.

'Your granddaughter is called Ruby,' he said gently.

But Cherry only shook her head, pulling her thin blankets around her frail frame. 'There no pickney inna dis home. We were never so blessed.' She turned away from him, looking out of the frosty window, a blank, sad look on her face.

The Doctor walked slowly out into the hall. His mind was racing, his chest tight. He felt as though he'd fallen from a great height and landed on his back, all the air pushed out of his lungs. Dizzy and disorientated; unable to tell up from down, left from right, or reality from… whatever *this* was.

As he walked back into the kitchen, Carla blinked at him. She *did* look confused, as though somewhere deep down, in a place growing further and further from her reach as every second passed… she knew something was wrong, something important was *missing*. But she couldn't put her finger on what.

Because this isn't your life! the Doctor wanted to shout.

'Who are you again?' she asked.

'I'm the Doctor, I—' He broke off. Above Carla's head, the ceiling was smooth. There was no crack to be seen. It had somehow… fixed itself. No. He turned back to look inside Carla's room. The window was pristine. Clear, faultless glass. And again – no ominous crack. The ceiling had closed up, like a body healing a wound in its flesh.

Everything is mending. Becoming solid, becoming permanent. This reality is growing stronger, rewriting memories, sealing the cracks.

Sealing Ruby out.

The Doctor was frantic now. He ran out of the room and burst into the kitchen. The ceiling was unblemished now throughout the whole house. He didn't know precisely what that meant, but he knew one thing for certain: *I'm running out of time.*

He looked Carla right in the eye, imploring her to remember. She was sat at the kitchen table, slumped, half-heartedly bouncing Lulubelle up and down. 'You had another child. Called Ruby.'

'I've never had children, mate.'

'No, you adopted her.'

Carla waved a hand, clearly frustrated. 'I *foster*. Now, don't be so stupid, I'm a foster-mother. I just do it now and then, that's all. All right? I've had maybe five or six kids.' She shrugged, as though if he'd asked her to, she wouldn't even had been able to recall their names with any certainty.

'No.' The Doctor shook his head, turning to the fridge, ready to point at all of Carla's postcards; the holiday photos; the Christmas cards from all over the country; the picture of Lulu and those of the other foster children, some shy, some excited; Ruby's school certificates and childhood drawings; photos of her as a little girl in her wellies with blonde pigtails, or in a swimsuit brandishing an ice cream.

But the fridge door was bare. Besides a few small magnets holding up a takeaway menu and some taxi firm cards, there was nothing but white metal. There was a hole in this house, a gaping void in the shape of a 19-year-old girl. All that was left behind was blank, empty space, filled with Carla's loneliness. Like a poisoned well.

The Doctor closed his eyes. It had really happened. The Goblins had done this. 'They've gone. The photos, and…'

'Who has gone?'

He looked at Carla, hoping she couldn't see the devastation behind his eyes. 'Your children. All those lives. Thirty-three, Carla.' He shook his head. *Not five or six.* 'You fostered thirty-three children. Children who needed you. And now, because of this… they've got no one. *Thirty-three*. What has happened to them without you?'

'Hah! How many?' Carla laughed in his face, showing some humour for the first time. 'Not me, darling! Don't be so stupid, that's too much like hard work. No way!' Her voice was firm, but her cheeks were pinched, her eyes cold. The Doctor was reminded that it was so much harder to be kind when life hadn't been kind to you. Happiness is like a spark – it catches. Ruby had been Carla's spark. But in this world, there was no Ruby. And Carla's spark had died, suffocated by the pressures of life.

In that same cold voice, Carla said, 'I'd never adopt. I just put my name on the list when I need a bit of money.'

'No, you don't.'

She wouldn't meet his eyes. 'Eight hundred quid per child.'

The Doctor closed his eyes. 'Don't say that.'

'I think you've got me mixed up with someone else,' Carla muttered, her voice drenched in bitterness. 'Cos there is no Ruby. There's just me. Stuck with my old mum. Up here in the attic.' Her eyes darkened. 'And I'm busy, anyway. I couldn't have a kid full-time. It would be a nightmare.' She held up Lulubelle, dangling her at arm's length, like she couldn't bear to be close with her. Like she didn't even care. 'And then this little brat arrives, ruining my holiday. I was looking forward to it. Christmas Day. Mum's asleep by three and I'll be all on my own, just how I like it. Why would I want a daughter? I'm happy as I am.' Tears glistened on Carla's cheek, falling steadily now, like little silver rivers in the cold kitchen light. 'I'm happy,' she said again, her voice cracking.

The Doctor shook his head. When he spoke, his voice was hoarse: 'Then why are you crying?'

'I don't know,' Carla said, her voice thick with tears. She looked up at him. 'Why are you?'

The Doctor grabbed the kitchen table, supporting himself against the tidal wave of grief threatening to subsume him. This was a violation of time. That crack hadn't just been a crack in the ceiling. It had been a crack in... in *everything*. In time and space. A crack in Cherry's heart – a dark, yawning void in Carla's soul. Big enough for a 19-year-old girl to fall through.

Or be snatched.

The Goblins had swallowed Ruby whole. Taken her whole life away, and ruined countless others in the process.

'They went back,' the Doctor murmured. Everything was sliding together in his mind, puzzle pieces slotting together. It was just as he'd said to Ruby during their conversation on the Goblin ship. The one that felt like years ago, now: *It's coincidences that stitch you in, that weave you into the day. All of it leading to a baby on Christmas Eve, same birthday as you.*

'They took the baby,' he said. 'The *other* baby.'

Carla stared back at him, face wet, uncomprehending.

'They cracked the timeline, but I will fix this.' *No time to lose.* He started walking toward the door. 'I will *fix* this.'

And then he was running. Barrelling out of the cold flat, with its empty fridge and its dusty spare room, and its oppressive, depressing quiet, and down the stairs. He leapt down them, taking two at a time, the dull thuds of his shoes hitting the creaky wood blurring with the sound of his own frantic heartbeats, both hearts, hammering like the Goblin drums. Kicking the front door open, he burst out onto the street, startling Ruby's elderly neighbour, and sprinting towards the TARDIS.

I know where I've got to go.

Chapter Seventeen

The sleek, white interior of the TARDIS was little comfort to the Doctor as he slammed the door and rushed towards the main console. His hands flew over the controls, yanking on levers and pushing buttons, his body on autopilot as his mind raced.

The date and time he was heading for was the only option he had for saving Ruby. But he had no idea what awaited him there, or if he would even be able to stop it from happening.

The haunted look in Carla's eyes flashed through his mind, as he launched the TARDIS away from London, the otherworldly sounds of its departure echoing throughout the chamber.

Hold on Ruby, I'm coming for you.

The TARDIS door creaked open. Snow flurried past the doorway in delicate white flakes, settling on the floor in a thick carpet, muffling all sound. A small village stretched out behind the police box, the warmly lit windows of the houses glowing like dozens of amber eyes.

In front of the TARDIS, visible through the doorway, was a road. And to the right, was a church with a small graveyard in front of it.

A retreating figure was just about visible through the falling snow. She shuffled down the laneway ahead like a pilgrim returning home, emptyhanded, penitent. Her shape was obscured by a bulky black cloak, the hood drawn up around her head against prying eyes.

The tears on the Doctor's face burned coldly in the chill of the night as he turned to look at the church, grand and imposing as an ancient giant sitting on the right side of the laneway, behind the hedges that lined the snowy path. The spire at the tip glinted knife-point silver in the faint gleam of the stars.

As he stepped out of the TARDIS, snow crunching underfoot, faint music reached him. Carols sung by choir boys, their high voices soaring, echoing against the vaulted ceiling of the church. The Doctor knew that song.

'Carol of the Bells.' The perfect song for Christmas Eve.

Narrowing his eyes, the Doctor brushed the tears from his face. Now was not the time for regret or fear. He was here to set things right. To save Ruby now, when she was just a baby, so he could save her future and the happiness of everyone she loved.

He had to act fast.

Scanning the sky, he sprinted towards the church. The Goblin ship had been easy to spot before, if you knew what you were looking for: abnormally dense cloud cover, or a dark, rainless storm that only seemed to cover a small area. But it was nighttime now, and the moon illuminated everything from above – he could see the ship, hovering in the clouds like a great, bloated dragon.

He raced through the graveyard, the sound of his footsteps mirroring the frantic beating of his hearts. If he couldn't locate the Goblins in order to stop them, he would just have to make sure he got to Ruby first.

Snow stung his eyes as he ran towards the church. The door was an outline of golden light, and in front of it was a small, wriggling shape. A shape with hands and feet—

Snicker-snacker.

'No!' The Doctor bellowed, as sneaky little hands darted out from the shadows, followed by the squat bodies of two Goblins in grubby, ripped trousers, grinning with razor-sharp teeth as they grabbed hold of the baby and snatched her off the church step.

They're changing history. They're going to eat Ruby and erase her from the timeline for ever. They're going to make it like she never even existed.

The Doctor charged forward.

The Goblins leapt upward, nimbly finding footholds in the stone walls of the church, and, scurrying toward the roof, seemingly impervious to the ice and the cold, cackling as they swung the baby to and fro. A wail sounded.

The Doctor didn't hesitate before easing open the heavy wooden door of the church and running inside. The Goblins were heading to the roof – no doubt that's where they would wait for the rope ladder to be lowered, and jump on, carrying Ruby away into the clouds, where they would season her up and feed her to their monstrous, alien monarch. The church was warm inside, his rapid footsteps muffled by the sound of the choir. But he barely noticed any of that as he slipped through the shadows, searching for a door, for some stairs to the roof—

There.

Quiet as a whisper, he darted through an open door at the back of the church. A flight of stone steps spiralled upward and he took them two at a time, the temperature dropping around him as he raced towards the roof, skidding round the corners, hauling himself upward, battling his own burning lungs, fighting against time itself and the creatures who sought to tear it to shreds and feast on the ruin they caused.

He burst out onto the roof in a flurry of snow. The sky was dark with clouds that roiled with thunder and something else – a black shape, gliding through the murky dark. *The ship.*

Movement caught his eye. The Goblins, a few metres away, up on a parapet, *just* out of reach, the rope ladder descending, and baby Ruby's basket already swinging its way towards the sky on a rope of its own. He was too late. The Goblins giggled as they jumped onto the rope ladder and began their skittering ascent toward the clouds. The end of the rope ladder dangled just out of reach as the Goblins raced up it, clearing rung after rung. Baby Ruby's basket was already growing smaller and smaller as the Doctor watched, helpless. Already, he could imagine the roar of jubilation inside the cobwebbed ship: a thousand slavering, hungry, alien mouths; drool puddling on the floor in anticipation of the feast of newborn flesh; the Goblin King, biggest and worst of all, his nose slits flaring with laboured breath, mouth open at the end of the conveyor belt; the mass of his slug-like body wobbling as he moaned, unable to contain his excitement. The eerie song they would all be singing. Distantly, he could hear them chanting, the roll of drums and the clash of the cymbals.

Oh, now we feast!
Oh, eat the beast!

Wind whipped the Doctor's coat around his legs, the full pockets clinking with all manner of things, but he barely noticed. He could jump up and climb the ladder, find his way back into the Goblin ship and save Ruby…

But that's what they'd done last time, and it hadn't worked.

That's why he was here, standing helplessly on the roof of the church on Ruby Road, nineteen years in the past, on Christmas Eve. Stealing Ruby back wouldn't save anyone – if the Goblins didn't eat something, they'd just ride through time and find someone else's life to ruin with accidents and clumsiness, and eventually write them out of it entirely. Who knew how many babies they'd already taken and eaten?

How many more victims there would be if he didn't put a stop to this macabre cycle. For ever.

I have to end this differently. There has to be another way. Think, Doctor, think!

His bulging pockets batted at him again.

'The gloves…' he murmured, and then suddenly he was tearing through his pockets, searching for the intelligent gloves. He grabbed them, shoving his hands inside before launching himself at the parapet. The rope ladder still dangled within reach.

Running a few paces, he launched himself into the air, arms outstretched, reaching up, up, up…

With a yell of triumph, the Doctor's hands closed around the final, gnarled wooden rung of the Goblin ladder. Vibrations juddered through his frame as he fell back to earth, feet connecting firmly with the stone floor of the parapet.

Golden light filled the sky around him as the gloves flickered on, and he heaved, straining as hard as he could.

If you reverse intelligent gloves, he'd said to Ruby – hours ago, nineteen years in the future, in a different life – *you get heavy.*

Chapter Eighteen

The rope halted in its upward progress, the Doctor grounding it like a 1,000-tonne anchor, holding down a titan-sized ship.

Fist over fist, the Doctor pulled the ship back down to the ground, grunting and yelling with exertion, muscles screaming in pain. He squeezed his eyes shut, locked his shoulders and *heaved* and, as he heaved, he thought about tiny baby Ruby and her precious little face, scared and confused, and how strong she would become, if only she were given the chance to live, to escape the Goblins and find Carla. *Oh, Carla*, he thought, gripping the rope with one hand over the other, still hauling the whole damned ship down. Carla with her vivacity and her warmth, her kindness and her amazing laugh, and the way she loved Ruby and her own mother, Cherry, unconditionally and completely. The way she loved them like there was nothing else that mattered in the whole world but her family.

That's the thing about family, about the people we love. When they go somewhere you can't follow, the whole world stops making sense. The entire universe becomes a stranger to you. And things which were so normal before, like fairy lights in the hall, and music on the radio... well, they might as well have vanished. You don't even notice them.

Life is meant to be shared, and some souls are meant to find each other. To share life with one another.

The Doctor yelled with the effort, sweat dripping down his forehead, down the back of his neck, rolling down his face and stinging his eyes, soaking his clothes. Snow melted on his skin, flushed with the force of his exertion. The hull of the ship dipped below the clouds, pitching to the side as he pulled. *Carla, Cherry, Ruby.* He chanted their names in his minds as he wrenched the entire Goblin ship closer and closer.

He couldn't let the ship leave. He had to keep it here, to stop it from sailing through time and claiming another victim.

In the corner of his eye, the spear-like spire of the church glinted in the moonlight, silver and wicked as a knife.

Harder and harder he pulled, and then the sails were visible, grey and thin as bat's wings, flapping in the snowstorm, waving as the Doctor wrenched the ship down. It felt like trying to pull the moon out of the sky, like trying to grab hold of a bus and slow it down with nothing but his bare hands and some hope.

The skeleton-like wires on the gloves grew brighter and brighter, gold light shining like he held a star in each hand, bristling with raw power. The rooftop of the church was lit up like it was daytime and, through the radiant flare, he saw the entirety of the Goblin ship shudder into view. It lurched downward through the snow clouds, its wooden wings spread out above it, like the galaxy's biggest vulture, descending on the small town.

The spire on top of the church was aligning with the hull, the metal cross on top it reflecting the light of the glove, so that the spire itself seemed to gleam with golden fire.

Nearly there.

The ship descended, jerking lower and lower as the Doctor bellowed with every rung he pulled closer to him, with every motion of his burning muscles. But it was *working.*

Almost there—

A shower of sparks singed the Doctor's skin as the gloves started to flicker out, fritzing and spitting energy, as he pushed them past their limit, desperate to see this through to the end, to extract all the energy he could from them, and more. He didn't have any other choice.

Cherry, he thought, and pulled. *Carla,* another pull. With a groan, he heaved once more.

Ruby.

It wasn't enough. In mere seconds the gloves would run out of charge and it would all be over. There was only one thing for it. Casting his gaze toward the nearby edge of the church roof, he tried to steady his laboured breathing. Nothing but empty space loomed past it.

Perfect, he thought. And then he jumped.

For a moment everything was still. Snow rushed past him, and the wind muffled all noise. He saw the whole of Ruby Road spread out before him, the dark night and the snow like a blanket over everything, families moving behind warmly lit and curtained windows.

And then he was falling, dropping like a stone through clear water, plummeting towards the floor, the ship following behind him, dragged down by his weight, made so much heavier by the intelligent gloves.

Immediately came the screeching sound of the jagged cross on top of the spire scraping along the bottom of the ship – a high-pitched, hair-raising sound, like steel on stone – before it smashed through the wood, piercing the boat.

And, the Doctor realised, as he heard a deep, groaning cry, *piercing the blubber of the Goblin King.*

He could imagine it clear as day, a bloodless death for a cruel giant, the spire staked through his heart like a vampire. The Goblins running around in chaos, instruments forgotten, eyes bulging in disbelief.

There was a moment of devastated quiet, in which the only sounds were the creaking of the ship as it fell to pieces and the last sputtering of the gloves as they finally ran out of power. The spire had halted the ship's progress, pinning it in place like a needle through a fat beetle. His fall was stopped short, the ground a short distance away. Finally, he was able to relinquish his grip on the rope ladder. Jumping to the ground, he allowed himself a single second to breathe, before craning his neck upward, looking for any possible sign of—

A basket was falling through the air like a comet, blankets billowing in the air, waving like white flags of surrender. The Doctor raced forward. Stumbling a little, he righted himself, reaching both hands out, stretching his tired arms forward like a net. He was just in time. The basket landed in his arms with a soft *thud*. Baby Ruby's newborn eyes blinked slowly up at him, and he became aware of the cold air and the choir, still singing 'Carol of the Bells' in the church. It had all taken less than four minutes.

The Doctor could've fallen to his knees right there in the snowy graveyard of the church on Ruby Road and cried in gratitude. He *hadn't* messed it all up.

Above him, something odd was happening to the ship. As he watched, it seemed to… fade. With every passing second, it grew less and less solid, less corporeal. Faintly, he could hear the despairing cries of the Goblins as a pale grey smoke swirled around their craft, as though erasing it from existence. *Or pulling it back into another world.*

Finally, the ship vanished.

Ruby sniffled, and the Doctor patted her forehead, giving her a little kiss on the cheek, fondness rushing through him.

'Happy Birthday, Ruby,' he whispered, before walking over to the front steps of the church and setting her down, tucking the blanket under her chin and around her tiny little ears. Closing the pattern, completing the loop. Restoring the order of events.

The clock atop the church began to chime, twelve tolls of the bell ringing out into the quiet Christmas Eve night. Midnight on Christmas Eve. The day was over – they were safe.

The Doctor took a deep breath, stepping back from the church. A feeling was spreading through him, prompted by the chiming of the clock, like several out-of-place organs were being put back in the right places. The constant hum of danger in the back of his mind slowly quietening down.

It was Time, clicking back into place. He had ejected the interference. And now? Business as usual.

The world spun on. That was not something to take for granted.

The Doctor turned back towards the TARDIS, walking out of the churchyard. Snow was falling more thickly, already covering his footsteps, vanishing them, just like the Goblin ship had vanished. It would be as if he'd never even visited Ruby Road.

The door to the TARDIS swung open when the Doctor pushed on it, and he stepped in, pausing in the doorway to look back at the church.

As he watched, the door creaked ajar, yellow light flooding out. A vicar stepped out, astonishment clear in his body language as he took in the small child bundled up in a basket, laid on his doorstep. After a moment he leaned down and picked up the basket, before turning quickly out of the cold, retreating inside.

The Doctor sighed with relief. *History, back on the right path.* He didn't know precisely what happened to Ruby after this – in between being found on the doorstep, and meeting Carla. But he had fixed the crack, sealed it up and triple-checked it. Ruby was back on her proper track. She was safe.

He was about to turn back into the TARDIS when he saw her.

The mother.

She was barely a silhouette in the rapidly falling snow, the haze of it blurring her figure so she seemed almost to flicker, about as real as a ghost. They were too far from one another to look each other in the eye, and her back was turned, but the Doctor felt watched nonetheless.

Did she see it all? Does she know what I did?

For a moment he thought he should go to her, ask her who she was. But something stopped him. *She left Ruby, that was her choice. I can't interfere any more.*

With that, he closed the door of the TARDIS, closing his eyes as he felt himself become untethered from Ruby Road, the police box melting away from the snowy street, and the church with its pointed spire and its graveyard.

With a sigh, the Doctor left Ruby Road behind.

Chapter Nineteen

The moment the TARDIS arrived on the Sundays' street, the Doctor was out of the door. He had to know if all he'd done had really worked.

He waved to Ruby's elderly neighbour, who had parked herself on her own porch in a foldout camping chair, as though she were watching the coming and goings of the TARDIS like it was a movie on an IMAX screen at the local cinema. As the Doctor bustled past, she took a swig from her hip flask and smacked her lips, waving cheerily back at him.

Pulling out his sonic screwdriver in a flash of blue and chrome, he pointed it straight at the door. A few buzzes later it was unlocked and swinging open, and he was bounding up the stairs. Without hesitation, he did the same to the front door of the flat, barging right in.

The crack in the ceiling had returned – back to how it had been, and *should be*, before the Goblins stole Ruby and changed everything. He didn't think he'd ever be so pleased to see such damage done to someone's perfectly nice flat. Slowly, cautiously he walked through the house. The spare room was no longer half-filled with sad odds and ends. It was Ruby's room again, messy but organised in the way only a teenage girl's bedroom can be.

Warm hope swelled in his heart. Music was playing, the sound of Christmas records filling the flat with cheer and twinkle. Somewhere in the house a voice was singing along – old but strong, and quite good.

Cherry! the Doctor thought. No longer a shadow of herself, but happy enough to sing.

And in the kitchen, the fridge – the fridge door! Crammed with photos once again, all those beautiful faces smiling out. Warm smells of Christmas cooking filled his nose, thyme and scotch bonnet mixing with nutmeg and all-spice, and the smell of roasting chicken. The fruity, brandy smell of Christmas cake underlying it all.

Then the Doctor stepped into the hall.

At the end of the corridor, Ruby in her red jumper and tartan shorts, cuddled up to Carla and Lulu, both of them smiling brightly, cheeks flushed with good cheer.

'There you are!' the Doctor said. He couldn't help it. He was so relieved and happy all at once. The burden was lifting off his shoulders. He grinned. 'Happy Birthday!'

'What happened to you?' Ruby asked. 'I turned round and … you were gone, or sort of like … well, I don't know, actually. Because I was here, and then … I got a bit lost. Or something.' Her brows were furrowed, the smile threatening to slip off her face. 'What happened?'

The Doctor waved his arms. *Where to start?* 'Lots of things! Because, well, they went *back*, didn't they? And you were *gone!* They went back and took you *as a baby*, so – so *I* went back, and—' He broke off. There was something he'd forgotten.

One more person to save.

'One moment,' he said.

The TARDIS took off and touched back down within moments. The Doctor stumbled out, breathless, into the poshest private hospital he'd ever seen. He scanned the room. *Where was she, where was she…?*

The tinkling of ornaments caught his attention. He whipped his head round, and there she was: Davina McCall, perched elegantly in a hospital wheelchair, half of her limbs stiff inside white casts, one hand holding a phone to her ear, as one of her assistants waited patiently nearby. The ornaments tinkled again, and the tree lurched dangerously, wobbling on its base. The spiky, pointed star glinted atop the tree.

Davina screamed.

The Doctor dived underneath the tree, just as it began to properly fall, catching it in one hand. Mission accomplished.

Davina paused mid-scream. She blinked up at him. Clearly terrified, and very confused as to where the tall, dark and handsome man in the long orange-brown leather coat had appeared from.

'You… you…' she stuttered. 'You saved my life.'

The Doctor winked. 'Merry Christmas, Davina McCall.'

The TARDIS reappeared on Ruby's street.

It had chosen a different position in front of the houses, but remained under the watchful eye of Mrs Flood, who took another long gulp from her hip flask just as the Doctor stepped out of the door.

What a day, he thought, weary and exhausted, as he walked up to Ruby's flat. Just before he reached the front door, his footsteps slowed and he paused.

How could he face them again? A happy family now, yes, but they so nearly hadn't been.

Because of him.

He stood outside the door, frozen. Everywhere he went, trouble seemed to follow. Everyone he befriended suffered in some way for having met him.

Behind him, Mrs Flood's voice came softly down the street. 'You're a busy man, aren't you, sweetheart?' she said. The Doctor turned to face her. She was smiling kindly, thin legs crossed over one another, hands clasped in her lap. 'You and your box of tricks. You look like you've lost a pound and found a sixpence. What's wrong?'

The Doctor searched for something funny to say that he could hide behind, or a joke that might distract her, and him, from the feeling washing over him like ice-cold water. In the end, he spoke before he realised what he was saying was the truth. 'I'm just wondering... Maybe I'm the bad luck.' A sigh. 'I think I'd better go.' He smiled tightly at Mrs Flood. 'Merry Christmas.'

She sat up in the chair, as if she hadn't been expecting him to leave for good so soon. 'Who are you anyway?' she asked.

The Doctor's smiled faded as he walked back toward the TARDIS. 'Oh, no one. I'm just passing by.'

'Well,' she said, just as the door of the TARDIS closed behind him with a soft *clunk*. 'You take care.'

But the Doctor didn't reply.

Chapter Twenty

Ruby finished stirring the condensed milk into her grandmother's tea – just how Cherry liked it, pale and syrupy sweet. She handed it to Carla, who walked down the hall and delivered it into her mother's wrinkled hands. Ruby heard the sound of Cherry kissing Carla on the cheek.

'Hallelujah, praise the Lord!' Cherry's voice echoed down the hall, making Ruby smile. 'I thought the day would never come. Mi tea reach at last!'

Ruby was baffled – where had the Doctor gone? He had burst into the house and then left just as quickly. Though to be honest, he was the least of their worries.

Carla came bustling into the kitchen. 'What are we supposed to do tonight?' she was muttering. 'This crack is like a wind tunnel! What are we supposed to do on Christmas Day? Sit here and freeze? Tuh!' She pursed her lips. 'And who is he anyway? That man, what's his name? Doctor what?'

Ruby was miles away, her mind still racing over the events of the last few hours. The last thing the Doctor had said to her before running off… 'What did he mean?' she murmured. 'That he went back?'

Carla tutted again, clearly frustrated.

Ruby could hardly blame her. A massive crack in the ceiling wasn't exactly something they could afford to get fixed just like that, and it was *freezing*. They couldn't move out either – the controlled rent on the apartment was so much cheaper than most flats in London, and Cherry would never leave this home, never mind the city itself.

'What sort of Doctor did he say he was, then?' Carla threw her hands up. 'Who the *hell* is he? And where on *Earth* did he come from? Why was he even here in the first place?'

'I don't know,' Ruby replied. 'He kind of popped up at the right moment, and then…' She frowned. 'Then he was gone. Like now.'

She paused, bracing her hands on the kitchen counter. Her mind was whirring, thoughts churning around like storm clouds, flashes of understanding like lightning in the murk of her confusion.

'It's been so mad, I haven't had time to stop and really think, but… he said I was taken as a baby.' Ruby looked up at Carla. 'Isn't that what he said, just now?'

Carla threw her hands up. 'I don't know, he's crazy—'

'Wait, no. Hush, hush, hush. Let me think. Because…' She closed her eyes, willing her brain to connect the dots. She felt that there was an answer out there to her questions, and if she could just reach far enough within her own mind and memories, she might grab hold. 'He went *back*? He said he went back… *Argh,* what does that *mean*—' Her eyes snapped open. 'When was Houdini?'

'What?'

'When was Houdini? He must have been alive in like, what? Nineteen-hundred? Nineteen-twenty? So how could they have spent a summer together…?' It all slotted into place at once, like the flashbulb of an old camera going off in her mind. One minute she didn't understand, and the next she did. 'He said he could take the baby out of the day. Out. Of the day. And he said about time travellers, he said – *oh!*'

Ruby didn't think about what she did next. She just knew she had to find him. Grabbing her jacket off the back of a chair, she pulled it on over her jumper, gave Carla a kiss on the cheek and ran out.

Sometimes extraordinary things bump against ordinary lives and change them, she thought as she ran down the stairs, Carla's shouts fading into the distance. *I have to find out if this is one of those extraordinary things. Or else I'll be thinking about it for the rest of my life. Always asking, what if?*

And I refuse to let that happen.

The front door was a rectangle of light, and she blew through it.

I refuse.

The street outside was empty except for Mrs Flood.

'Mrs Flood,' Ruby gasped, breathless. 'Did you see anyone? There was a man. This tall, and… *amazing.* Wearing a big leather coat?'

The old woman nodded sagely to the blue police box.

'What d'you mean?' Ruby looked at the box. Then, with a tingle in her spine, she realised it had shifted position.

Closer to her flat.

Ruby walked closer, until she was just a few paces away. From this distance she could see the grain of the wood, the blue paint. The glass at the top, and the dust in the corners of the panes.

As she watched, the door cracked ajar, creaking open. And light flickered from inside. A chill went down Ruby's spine. She wasn't scared but, now that she looked – really looked – at the box, there was something about it she couldn't put her finger on. An energy she could feel but not describe. She looked back at Mrs Flood, who shrugged, a small smile tugging at the corners of her mouth.

Ruby pushed open the door and walked in.

In that one moment – between her opening the door, looking around, trying to understand what she was seeing and walking straight back out – everything changed. Or maybe it had already. Maybe it all changed the moment she saw the Doctor dancing in the strobing lights of the club. Maybe that was what rewrote her reality.

The door of the police box slammed shut behind her as she stumbled back out onto her street. She stood with the box to her back, eyes wide, staring blankly at the houses ahead. What she had just seen ... it couldn't be *real*.

Turning back to the box, she ran her hands over it, fingertips trailing along the smooth blue varnish of the wood. The topography of the panels beneath her hands were at once familiar and altogether alien, now that she knew what they concealed. The vastness of all they held inside. The sound of her own heartbeat thudded through her ears, as she walked around the whole thing in a slow circle, trying to discern the trick, to reveal the illusion. But the box remained a box, with a handle and a lock, and those small square windows with their frosted glass.

She paused. Became aware again of her surroundings, as the wonder and the disbelief began to turn to something stronger.

Curiosity.

From across the street, Mrs Flood met her eyes. 'Good luck, Ruby.' Her voice was quiet, but it carried, and something flared to life in Ruby's heart, like a match touched to wood.

I've been waiting, all this time, for my life to begin, Ruby thought, as she stretched out her hand. *Nineteen years. Maybe it's time to stop waiting.*

Maybe it's time to start living.

Underneath her hand, the door of the police box swung open, and she stepped inside.

Epilogue

The sound of ancient engines echoed through the residential London street, the oscillating noise rising and falling as the TARDIS faded in and out of view. The engines gave one last heave and, as quickly as it had arrived, the big blue box vanished, taking Ruby Sunday with it.

Across the road, Mrs Flood nodded, smiling to herself, and stood up, folding her chair and tucking it under one arm. *Enough excitement for one day,* she thought.

The sound of footsteps slapping against concrete caught her attention. It was Abdul, racing down the street, a bewildered look on his face.

'But…' he said. 'Did you see that?' He turned to her, eyes wild. She tried not to let her amusement show on her face. 'Mrs Flood, did you see? The box thing – it just *vanished!*' He looked back at the street, blinking hard. 'It was there, and then it wasn't. It just disappeared. I *saw it* disappear—'

Mrs Flood just waved a hand. She and Abdul rarely saw eye to eye, but she liked him really. 'Oh, merry Christmas, Abdul,' she tutted. 'Stop making such a fuss.'

Still frowning in confusion, he left, cursing his difficult neighbour, and muttering about the supernatural capabilities of blue police boxes. When he was gone, Mrs Flood allowed a sly smile to break out over her face.

'What?' she whispered to herself when he was safely out of earshot. 'Never seen a TARDIS before?'